THE SECOND FIVE

By
Raymond Maher

Raymond Maher
Dec. 11, 2022

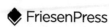 FriesenPress

One Printers Way
Altona, MB R0G 0B0
Canada

www.friesenpress.com

Copyright © 2022 by Raymond Maher
First Edition — 2022

Editor: Eden Maher

ISBN
978-1-03-914846-8 (Hardcover)
978-1-03-914845-1 (Paperback)
978-1-03-914847-5 (eBook)

1. FICTION, HISTORICAL

Distributed to the trade by The Ingram Book Company

INTRODUCTION

THE SECOND FIVE reflects the words of Alexander the Great, "Remember, upon the conduct of each depends the fate of all."

The story is about the destiny of five partners searching for gold along the Fraser River in British Columbia in 1860. We see the curious circumstances that connect the men for good and evil. On their journey, events beyond their control shift like the elusive gold they seek.

The book is a work of fiction but reflects actual historical events and individuals. The fictional characters challenge readers to understand their motives for being caught up in the gold rush and the daringness of their search.

In its predecessor, *The Deadly Five*, the search for gold began in 1859. The five men were among a torrent of thousands of gold seekers rushing to the Fraser River and Canyon for the placer gold being found in the gravel bars of the river. They had success getting gold but the misfortune of being labeled the Deadly Five. Approaching winter forced them to halt their search.

In *The Second Five*, the quest resumes for those willing on April 11, 1860, at Fort Hope on the Fraser River.

Not all of the original five partners can continue in the second search. The second five partners are three old and two new. That is, three experienced and leery, and two men eager for the adventure ahead of them. Nothing Brown, Mean Mike, and Jacque are the seasoned men who know the difficulties of their task. On the other hand, Henry Arden and CF are eager and prove that they cannot be intimidated by what comes their way.

The Second Five can be read and enjoyed as a stand-alone book without reading *The Deadly Five*. However, those willing to read both books will find it is like wearing two socks instead of one.

CHAPTER ONE:
At the Starting Line

A FAREWELL LETTER to Popcorn Pete and One-Foot-Charlie delivered to the infirmary of the Royal Engineers, New Westminster, British Columbia

April 9, 1860

Dear Pete and Charlie,

I'll not say good-bye, for I am sure we will meet again. Pete, you have a gift for surgery and will be a great asset to the Royal Engineers when your training is complete. Charlie, your friendship with Pete is inspiring, and you will help him adjust to his training in England. I will not forget how you both could accept any situation with patience and good humor.

As I need more time to come to terms with my willingness to operate on people, I am off to search once more for gold. While doing so, I will decide if I have the nerve, toughness, stomach, and backbone that surgery demands of a doctor.

You know most of our new group of gold seekers: Mean Mike, Jacque, Henry Arden, and me. Claude, a young friend of Jacque, is

the only one unfamiliar to you. I hope this time we are not branded as the Deadly Five.

I'll miss you both exceedingly. Till the three of us are together again, may God be gracious to each of us.

Best Regards,

Nothing Brown

After dropping off my letter for Popcorn Pete and One-Foot-Charlie at the infirmary of the Royal Engineers in New Westminster, British Columbia, I took a steamer to Hope. Arriving there on April 10, a day before our full group was to gather for our new search for gold, Jacque and Claude met me. Jacque was my partner and friend from our first gold hunting group. As a former fur trader for the Hudson's Bay Company, he was aware of fur trading trails and skilled in canoe river travel in the Pacific Northwest. Jacque had brought a young companion named Claude for our second gold expedition. Together, they had already retrieved our equipment, which we had stored last fall, as well as our two canoes.

On a sliver of land along the Fraser River, they had set up a camp for our gathering near Fort Hope. When set up, our two tents occupied most of the space. Towering pine and cedar trees and steep rocky cliffs bordered the campsite. Jacque and I talked long into the night, but Claude offered only a few words, then turned in early. He and Jacque were up before dawn, and I struggled awake with the rising sun.

April 11, 1860, the long-planned day of our rendezvous, began with the pale, yellow sun breaking through wispy white clouds encircling the higher reaches of the mountains at Hope. A damp chill assaulted everything. The morning was still and silent except for the sound of the rushing river consumed with itself. I drank the strong black tea that Jacque had placed in my hand. He and Claude had left the camp for the Hudson's Bay Company fort to meet up with Mean Mike. Henry Arden was to join us around noon.

Without any squawking or scolding, a solitary crow landed nearby and stared at me with piercing eyes, as if he wanted to give me a piece of his mind. "Look, friend," I told the bird, "I'm not going to disturb you. I'll be pushing on shortly with my partners, up the Fraser searching for gold. If you recognize me from last summer, it might be because Old Man Magee was popular with you crows for leaving fish guts on the ground for you to eat. Old Man Magee was a fine fisherman, but he won't be with us this time. We laid him to rest in his grave, the victim of a jealous husband. He lies in his grave near Seph, another one of our first group. Seph died from sickness. Last time, they slandered our group as, 'The Deadly Five,' but I suspect you don't care one way or the other about what we were called."

I paused to drink my tea before it got cold, and the crow made no effort to leave or discourage me from continuing to bend his ear. "Yes, Mr. Crow, The Deadly Five has shrunk to the three of us, but we have added two new men, so we are now The Second Five. Will you wish us luck?"

The crow just sat staring at me like he was sent to listen. It was a welcome change. Many others might ignore me. My name, Nothing Brown, was given to me by clueless individuals who judge others solely by outward appearances. Not many are waiting with unwavering attention to hear a short guy like me. I have no deep or commanding voice or exuberant liveliness that attracts attention. A lack of height should not be my obsession. I am not the only short person in this world, but I have never been comfortable with my boiled-down size. Do others dismiss those who are short? Probably not as much as I feel that they do. It's humbling to consider that even if I was tall, others might still ignore me. Character makes the man, but there is always great division about who is being celebrated or rejected in spite of their character or lack of it.

Since the crow did not attempt to leave me to talk to myself, I kept talking to him, so I could push back the wilderness that was closing in around me. Having been away for the harsh winter at New Westminster, I realized once again how intimidating, overwhelming, oppressive, and suffocating it could seem to me at times. The supremacy of the mountainous wilderness was said to rule from Fort Hope and onward up the Fraser River.

I asked the crow, "Do you know why five is the right number for a partnership between men?" Without giving the bird a chance to respond, I continued talking. "With a partnership of two men, they may turn against each other in a difference of opinion and go their separate ways. If there are three men, there will always be two against one to solve an issue between them, leading to resentment. A partnership of four men may well become two against two and leave issues without satisfactory resolutions.

A group of five becomes a working combination like the five points of a star. There are five points to a human body, which are two feet, two hands, and one head. The head is needed to direct the feet and hands. Five men together force one to act as the head when decisions need to be made. Whoever will serve as the leader must be able to get two others on his side for solving any issue."

The crow flapped his wings and stood on one foot as I finished my ramblings. It seemed that I had wasted my breath, as the bird still seemed uncommitted to all my words. It suddenly dawned on me that the crow was listening to me in the hopes that I would offer him some food. I pulled off a chunk of sourdough bread from my food pack and threw it at the bird's feet. To my surprise, he began to pick at the bread without greediness or exaggerated eagerness, as if he had been taught good table manners before he met me.

"That crow with me," Claude stated pointing at the bird, then back at himself. He had returned to the campsite on soundless feet, and I had not seen or heard his arrival. It felt like he had materialized out of nowhere.

I said in a startled voice, "Claude, you are like Jacque, who also appears beside me, but I never see or hear him coming either."

"You not see, or hear, me either. I fox spirit. I no Blue Jay, whole forest hear and see him."

I wondered why this young man would be friends with a crow, but

I assumed it may have something to do with being part Native like Jacque. My perceptions of Native people were that they had a keen knowledge of birds, animals, and nature for hunting for food. I did not think that they had pets except for dogs, and I was told they ate their dogs if they were starving. I asked Claude, "Why is this crow with you?"

"I help crow as friend. He flies only little way with one poor wing. I give crow food. He safe near me."

"Your spirit is fox. Are they friends of crows?"

"Not friends. Crow with me, as crow smart like me, fox."

"I wonder which animal would be my animal spirit. You don't know me yet, so I'll ask you after you know me better."

"Jacque says you rabbit, but you act like porcupine throwing quills when you want. Jacque says Mean Mike loud rooster crowing, and he wants fight."

"I like being both a rabbit and a porcupine. I can run away fast as a rabbit and also stand and fight fearlessly as a porcupine. Mean Mike is only a loud rooster when he's drunk. Does Jacque also say that you are a fox spirit?"

"Jacque says I fox, or coyote. He tell me one respected, one scorned. Both have slyness, but only fox respected."

Realizing that Claude and I had been talking for some time, I asked him, "Where is Jacque? Did you find Mean Mike at the fort?"

"Yes, we meet Mean Mike. Now Jacque and Mean Mike get supplies for trip. Jacque send me back here get firewood, fish, hunt."

"I'll get firewood, so you can hunt or fish as you want. I'll be going to the fort at noon to meet Henry Arden."

"Why meet Henry Arden? To help him?"

"No, Henry doesn't need my help. He's my good friend and new to our group like you. I want to welcome him. He and Mean Mike had a fight once, and I don't want there to be friction between them."

"Is friction another fight?"

"Friction might lead to a fight because they don't get along well together. They do not like each other. I like both Mean Mike and Henry, and I'll try to keep them from aggravating each other!" I explained, not realizing I was being as clear as mud to Claude.

"Is aggravating the same as annoying?" Claude asked eagerly, hoping to hear me say something that made sense to him.

"Yes, aggravating means they annoy, irritate, provoke, or anger each other," I answered.

"I know about anger. Which one have bigger anger, Henry or Mike?" Claude said with a grin.

"Both men are good fighters and can show anger," I responded. "Mean Mike picks fights if he has been drinking. When Mike is sober, he's pretty easy to have a good relationship with. Henry is always an agreeable person but will not back down to Mike or anyone who wants an altercation. Both men are great if we need to fight. Henry is a good boxer. Mean Mike is strong but moves slowly because of his size."

"Jacque says you mad dog when you fight. Scream, flop on the ground, bark like dog, bite. Jacque says hunting gold not much about fighting. He says that it mostly hard work to get gold."

"Jacque is right. Hunting for gold is difficult work. But sometimes we will have to fight. Do you like to fight?"

"If I win," Claude said slyly.

"Winning is better than losing," I declared, laughing. "I'll get collecting firewood, so you can fish and hunt."

"I show you where dead tree for much firewood," Claude offered.

"Well, lead the way so we get something done before noon," I said, following the young man heading for a dead tree.

The morning passed with me gathering a large supply of firewood and Claude hunting away from camp. He had not returned to the campsite when I left for Fort Hope. There were a formidable number of gold seekers around the fort. Supplies there were expensive, but sales were fast flowing. I made slow progress in finding my partners. At last, I saw Mean Mike, a head taller than most of the surging crowd, with a saloon girl on his arm.

When Mike spotted me waving at him, I knew he had been drinking, as he yelled like thunder, "Nothin', how the hell are ye lad?"

The next thing I knew, I was lifted off the ground and hugged in his tree-limb arms. Releasing me to the ground from his bear hug, he announced with a silly grin, "This here be the very love of my life, Miss Violet, from the Nugget Saloon."

"Pleased to meet you, Violet. Are you leading Mike away from the saloon before he causes more fights?"

"It was that, or have no saloon left to go back to," Violet said laughingly with a pretty smile. I wondered, did Mike pick the pretty girls, or did they pick him? All I knew was that Mike had lots of them on his arm as long as I had known him.

I asked Violet, "Could I borrow Mike from you, as he has some business to attend to with his partners?"

Violet winked at me, stretched up and kissed Mike on the cheek, and said, "See you later, hon." She was gone before Mike could object.

"Where's Jacque?" I asked Mike, who stood waving a bit in tipsiness, watching Violet disappearing from his sight. After a long moment, Mike was able to focus enough to answer.

"He's with the canoe and the supplies we bought. He's close enough to see steamers unload their passengers and watching for Henry Arden to get here."

"Why didn't you wait with him?" I prodded.

"We had a few words this morning," Mike sullenly admitted. "I didn't take to Jacque's young friend, who often gives me one-word answers." Mike continued sullenly, "I asked Jacque why the young lad couldn't carry on a conversation in English. To which he said that his mother's tribe had mostly raised him. I said that the boy should join us when he could speak more English. Jacque said that I talked too much, and his friend would be a welcome change to my continual yapping. Jacque sent the lad back to camp and warned me not to be mean to the boy, as he would be watching me. I told Jacque to quit acting like he was the lad's old man. Jacque told me to have a drink and leave him alone. Which I did, and there I met the lovely Violet."

"It has been a while since we have had to work together and get along, Mike. Jacque wants his young friend accepted, and for us to give him a chance. You are right in that at first it seems hard because Claude is overly quiet, but it didn't take me long to get more words out of him this morning. He is shy, but I have good feeling about him. Old Man Magee had smelly socks that caused a bear to move on upriver last time, so I'm sure we can overcome a little limited English this time.

Didn't you get some of your steam let off at the saloon?" I asked Mike.

"I did have a few fights there, and I'm ready to say I'm sorry to Jacque, so let's go see him."

"Before we do, let me know if you can be tolerable to Henry? I don't want you also fighting with him."

"Nothin', don't keep pestering me!" Mike said, ignoring answering my question. He changed the subject with, "The steamers be delayed today. I'll lead the way, as I know where Jacque be waitin' beyond the dock."

Mike led me through the crowd of men coming and going to and from and beyond the fort. I almost bumped into Mike as he stopped for a string of mules ladened with packs of supplies. A few men were on horseback, but mostly everyone was on foot, intent on going somewhere in this piece of so-called civilization beside the river that promised gold.

The dock area was empty of any steamers, and we found Jacque beside the canoe, holding the supplies. Jacque was as cool as frost to Mike, and I suspected Mike had left some crucial details out of his account of their argument. It looked like we might be starting on a bumpy partnership, but a whistle had us all looking at a tall figure of a man hailing us and coming toward us. The three of us broke out into glad smiles. It was Judge Matthew Begbie.

CHAPTER TWO:

From the Past to the Unravelling Present

THE TENSION THAT had held each of us melted as Judge Begbie advanced toward our group, standing beside the river and our canoe. His greeting, "Three of my favorite gold hunters," was warm and sincere. "Jolly good to see each of you again. I assume you're searching for gold. The blessing of Old Man Magee and Seph are with you, I'm sure. Are your new partners able to adjust to you and your ghosts?" The judge said this all-in-one unending breath. We remembered he was a long-winded rambler, seldom waiting for anyone to respond to him.

"We don't have no damn ghosts," Mean Mike uttered belligerently. Jacque sighed loudly and deeply, but the judge laughed at Mike's reply.

"What I'm saying is that Old Man Magee was one of a kind, and he steadied your group. His beautiful singing and violin playing tamed the wilderness for you. Seph was a quiet giant, as quiet as Mike is loud. You had two very steady blokes. Who are your new partners, or is it now a partnership of three?"

"I have a young friend named Claude, who is a seventeen-year-old Native. He is my partner, and he will be one to the others—if they will accept him,' Jacque said, looking stonily at Mean Mike.

I spoke up quickly, "Judge, you know our other new partner, Henry Arden, from New Westminster."

"Indeed, I do, a fine fellow of character and pedigree. Your new singer and bearer of musical talent. He sleeps with his pitch pipe and will have you learning a choir piece while digging for gold. By Jove, it will be such a grand treat to meet up with you again, as I hold court in this gold rush country. Do you suppose, chaps, that we could meet for supper this evening here at Hope?"

"The Golden Nugget Saloon offers a meal of beef stew and hot biscuits," Mean Mike said with enthusiasm.

"We are waiting for Henry to arrive on a steamer, and Claude is at the camp, so could we meet around six?" I asked the judge.

`Judge Begbie pulled out his pocket watch, looked at it, and said, "That is the verdict. I will see you at the Golden Nugget at six or slightly later."

As our acquaintance walked away, the three of us said at once, laughingly, "Slightly later can mean anything with the judge."

Mean Mike asked if we could sit down before he fell, so we sat on the ground, facing each other.

"Jacque, I have a big mouth. I didn't realize the Indian lad was an important friend of yours. You know I say stuff that causes trouble. I'm sorry, but I cannot promise it won't happen again," Mean Mike stated honestly.

"Mike, I'm going to level with you. Claude is not my friend but my son. I was not going to say we were father and son, but I see it is better if everyone knows." Jacque's eyes were searching Mike's face for his reaction. I watched Mean Mike's expression also, hoping for a response that wouldn't be foolish or cruel. Mike could be both thoughtful with his words and cluelessly offensive.

Mike looked like a light went off in his head, and he said, "No wonder you were ready to punch me when I insulted Claude's English." Mike held up his hands, shrugging, and continued, "Forget what I said, Jacque, I was an ass."

Jacque went on to explain, "Claude is caught between the White and Native worlds because of me, his father. So far, he has lived in the world of his mother, my wife, who works at the Hudson's Bay Company fort at Kamloops. Her people are the TK'emlups, often referred to as the Shuswap Indians by the White, who struggle with native names. Claude is his baptized name, but he is called Little Fox by his mother's people. I have had little time with him, or influence. His mother is willing to let him learn more of my world, as he is almost a man. I do not know how to be more than a father from a distance. It is hard for both Claude and me. We are strangers to each other in so many ways," Jacque said humbly, as if he was carrying a heavy burden.

Mike missed the complexity of Jacque's situation and the diffi-culty of parenting. He said to Jacque, "Me and Nothin' will help ye father yer son. I can teach him how White men drink and fight. Nothin' can teach him the kindness of Quakers and more English. This Henry Arden who's coming can teach him the manners of British nobility and singin'. When we're done with him, he'll be a kind and mannerly fellow, who speaks good English, can fight and drink like an American Scotsman like me, and is able to take care of himself."

Jacque just rolled his eyes and shook his head at Mike. How simply Mike regarded the challenge before him. Mike did not grasp the difficulty of being of mixed blood. It could be the best of two ancestries or cut off and rejected by both. His wife and her family had raised Claude well. He was familiar with the work and trade that went on at the fort, but he was also well trained in the Native life that had no connection to it. How could Jacque help him thrive in both the White and Native worlds? Most of all, how could he show his son his love for him?

I wanted to tell Jacque I understood about not fitting in as a Quaker and that acceptance is never easy for anyone. I decided that Jacque didn't need us to say anything to him, and I should keep my opinions to myself and let him speak his mind. I had no doubt Jacque would be a good father to his son. It would just be a matter of time and learning how by doing the best he could when and as he could.

The afternoon sun had a penetrating warmth as we continued to sit on the ground and talk. Maybe because Jacque had been so open with us, I surprised myself when I said, "Guys, I have to be honest. I am struggling to get enthusiastic and motivated for this second trip. Everything was new and exciting the first time. This expedition seems different to me. I am remembering overturned canoes, endless rain, and mud, being chilled to the bone, cold hands, wet feet and clothes, mosquitoes, black flies, skunk spray, bears, dead men, and people that mistrusted and hated us. Didn't we have enough adventure last year to last a lifetime?"

Both men looked at me as if I had offended or shocked them with my words. The silence was deafening, but at last, Mean Mike said, "Truth be told, I've had second thoughts too. It's easier to go blindly ahead into the unknown than to have a sound idea of what you're in for the second time around. I've heard finding gold in the Fraser Canyon, where we're heading, may be far more difficult than what we experienced last time. That probably doesn't make ye feel better, Nothin'."

Mike then added with honest conviction, "The way I see it, all we ever have to endure is one day at a time whether good or bad. The three of us know we can trust each other with our lives no matter what we find ahead."

Jacque said with a rare grin, "I've have had some second thoughts too, but Claude is so excited to travel with me and my trusted friends, to find gold, to see and explore the wilderness beyond his home. I've told him it's hard work. If I let him know there will be overturned canoes, endless rain and mud, and all the other things you mentioned, Nothing, he would say, 'That not new to me!' We have one partner excited enough for all of us."

"Not just one, we have two partners who are eager about our journey. Henry Arden is busting at the seams to be able to search for gold with us," I said. Then I was surprised at myself again, saying, "I guess that I need to get my mind off our first trip and move on to the second one, with Claude and Henry and you two left-overs. The memory of Old Man Magee and Seph will always be bittersweet, and I will always honor them, but only a fool gets stuck on yesterday. It is time for me to stop focusing on the past and doubting myself and get on with our emerging future."

"What mean ye, laddie, by emerging?" Mean Mike said playfully in his exaggerated Scottish accent, which he used from time to time to remind us of his true Scottish blood.

"The future is unravelling about us as I speak, Mikey," I said in reply.

Jacque stood, stretched, and offered a hand up to Mike. Instead of taking it as an aid to his feet, Mike pulled on Jacque's hand to pull him down. Jacque was ready for Mike, who could always be counted on to play a trick on anyone. Still being a little drunk, Mean Mike was slow in putting his whole strength into his pull, and Jacque tugged him forward a couple of feet on the ground, and then let go. It was like pulling a horse, but Jacque was up to the challenge for a couple of feet to best Mike at his own game.

"Damn," said Mike, "I should have known ye'd be ready for me."

"Come on," exclaimed Jacque, "Let's take the supplies in the canoe to the camp, and then we'll be back with Claude and the other canoe by six."

"What about Nothin'?" Mean Mike asked as he got to his feet.

"He'll wait for Henry and also heal the sick or hold a prayer service," Jacque said, teasing me about being a lay preacher and a man who did doctoring when and where needed.

My partners appreciated my efforts in these two regards, but we badgered each other good naturedly as a bit fun. I was not a blood and thunder preacher who threatened people with God. Instead, I focused on the life and teachings of Jesus. I respected the faith beliefs—or disbelief—of my partners and everyone who became part of our gold search. I did my best to help the sick and injured, as trained doctors were rare in the wilderness. I had my heart set on becoming a fully trained physician in time. I had worked with an educated and licensed Royal Engineers' doctor during the winter at New Westminster.

"I'll do them both," I said, then added, "we'll be here waiting for you."

I watched the canoe with Jacque and Mike disappear from sight down the river. Then I pulled out my pocket Bible that I always carried with me and began reading from my favorite book of the Old Testament. When I was nearly through, the whistle sounded to announce the arrival of a steamer at the dock.

I stood up and watched carefully as the passengers disembarked. I walked closer to those abandoning the ship and spotted Henry Arden. He had a large backpack and one satchel. In his flannel shirt, corduroy jacket, and pants, Henry was similar to a multitude of gold seekers geared up for their advance into the wilds.

Henry had changed in the few months he had been in the new British colony of British Columbia. A handsome man of better than average height, Henry arrived at New Westminster looking and dressing like a British gentleman of birth and nobility. In a frontier society, he soon learned that his family name and country estate meant nothing to anyone except a bar maid interested in the amount of his old money in England. He had shared the truth with me that his family's fortune was running desperately low. The ancestral estate, which dated back to the Norman Conquest, might end up for auction before many more years. Like so many others in the gold rush, he hoped to strike it rich and shore up crumbling family wealth. Henry had shown me he was intelligent, adaptable, trustworthy, and expected no special treatment other than what he earned or deserved.

"You're a sight for my sore eyes," Henry called as I approached him. I held out my hand for a proper British handshake. Henry surprised me with a friendly hug

"Sorry we limped in here late. There was the sound of a small explosion this morning, then there was smoke rising from below the deck. The crew extinguished the fire, but there was one casualty among them. My eyes are still burning from the smoke. Can you smell it on me and from the boat?" Henry asked.

"I thought it was your cologne, but I am sorry for the mishap on your ship. Glad you are here unharmed."

"I'm glad to be safe and sound, but not all men were unscathed. I hope you have your little doctor kit with you, as I suggested you might help a couple of passengers who got cut with flying glass due to the explosion." He then went on to explain, "There was a doctor on board, but he was busy with several people more seriously hurt. I wrapped their wounds; one is not serious, but the other is more so. If you cannot help them, we'll need to take them to a doctor if there is one here."

"Yes, I have my small kit with me. You know I'll help them if I can."

Henry nodded approvingly and said, "They're waiting near the gangplank, so I'll bring them to you." Then he quickly made his way to them and led them back to me.

My training and experience in doctoring kicked in as I said, "Let's get closer to the river, so I can get some clean water to cleanse the cuts. Henry, if you have a pan in your pack and salt, I will need them both. Fellows, I do treatments, but I'm not a fully trained doctor. Do you want me to attend to your cuts?" The two men nodded their heads. "Who should I start with?" I asked Henry.

"This chap has a piece of glass embedded in his right arm. I was afraid to pull it out in case I could not stop the bleeding," Henry said, bringing a tall man with a bloody rag wrapped about his arm over to me.

"Look away from your wound or close your eyes," I told the man. "Henry, have clean water in your pan with salt in it. When I pull the glass out, pour the water over the wound on his arm," I directed. Then I turned back to the man and explained, "Sir, the salty water is to cleanse your wound to help prevent infection. After the water, I'll stitch your arm up. Last thing, I'll apply iodine on the wound. Keep your arm lightly covered with clean long-sleeve shirts while it heals."

Thankfully, the shard of glass was not deep, but it did take five stitches to close the cut. The man was pleased with the light orange-brown color of iodine on his wound. While I had stitched him up, Henry had dealt with the other man, who had instinctively covered his face with his hands in the flying glass. The backs of his hands had numerous small cuts, but none needed stitches. Having worked with me doctoring many times before, Henry had the man soak his hands in salty water, and then he applied iodine to the cuts. We walked the two men back to the dock, and then they left us with their thanks. We stood at the mostly empty dock near the steamer. Henry said that treating the two men was just like helping me doctor at the saloon.

"It could be really busy at times there," I said in agreement. "I am sure glad to have you along on this search for gold," I stated sincerely.

I remembered our plans for the evening and alerted Henry. "By the way," I said, "we are having supper tonight with Judge Begbie, who ran into us here this afternoon. I hope you are in good voice because the judge remembers you as a choir director. He is always eager to show off his operatic talent and get everyone singing with him. The judge prophesied that you would have us learning choir music while we dig for gold. In fact, he said you sleep with your pitch pipe."

"Eck gads! My scandal is revealed. Such a dastardly deed to sleep with a pitch pipe and have it made public knowledge. Please, Nothing, don't dismiss me as a worthless cur," Henry said mockingly.

"No dismissal for you, as long as you vow to keep that pitch pipe well hidden. You must promise on your honor not to corrupt anyone in our group with that vile thing," I insisted seriously.

"I promise on all the bread and butter in England. If that is not enough, I'll throw in all tea and ale there too," Henry said pleadingly.

"I think we have taken this conversation quite far enough. Let's talk about Claude, who is Jacque's son. You know the rest of us, but Claude is a young Native who is shy and speaks a limited number of English words. It can be an adjustment to talk with him, so I'm giving you a heads up for tonight."

"I know how Claude feels. Many have trouble with my English accent, and I hate hearing people say, 'I don't understand what you said, or slow down there, governor, and say that again.'"

I wanted to say that it wasn't really the same situation with Claude, but I let it go. Presently, since we were still on the deck, we saw two crewmen carry out a dead body on a stretcher. The body was wrapped in a thin sheet that blew about in the breeze as it was lain on the deck. The men stood somberly beside it. The captain of the steamer joined them, carrying a shovel, and asked if we could point them to the graveyard. We couldn't tell them but directed them to inquire at the Hudson's Bay Company store close to the dock.

As we watched them head off, Mike appeared, calling to us in a sober and anxious voice. "I came to get ye, as we can't find Claude. Jacque is looking for the lad, and he sent me to bring you back to camp to help search." We quickly departed with Mike and made good time, rowing the canoe to our camp. It would allow Henry a chance to place his backpack and satchel in our basecamp. I was certain Claude was fine and just busy hunting or fishing, out of sight.

Jacque met us as we came ashore and indicated there was still no sign of Claude. I asked Jacque if he had looked for the boy's crow because the bird kept close to him. We were in the group talking when Claude appeared suddenly beside us, saying, "Good you here. I drag a small deer here. It's bled. It needs to be skinned and gutted. I go fish now. Nothing already bring much firewood." We looked at each other and grinned. Jacque looked both relieved and proud.

We set to work skinning the deer, and Henry excitedly joined in, which surprised Mean Mike. We still arrived back at the fort by six for supper, not surprised to find Judge Begbie was not there. We ate our stew, knowing he would arrive sometime later.

It was during our meal at the Golden Nugget Saloon that we learned Claude resented his name, as it was not a Shuswap one and made him marked by his people as part White. I suggested he go by the initials CF. C for Claude, and F for Fox. When asked his name, he could say, "Call me CF." If they wanted to know what the letters stood for, he could say Claude Fox. I told him that it would work well in a White world, and with his own people, he could just say, "I Fox, not Little Fox, now."

Claude said with satisfaction, "I now CF in White world. You call me CF not Claude." We clapped and shouted our approval, then waited patiently for the judge.

CHAPTER THREE:
Getting Down and Muddy

THE GOLDEN NUGGET Saloon was one of several such establishments near the Hudson's Bay Company Fort at Hope. It was a bit more polished than some others in that it was better than a big tent with a plank floor. The Nugget was a wooden structure with a distinctively large Dutch entrance door. When only the top half of the door was open in the morning, a simple breakfast could be purchased with coffee or tea, and the meal came with a slice of fresh baked bread.

A shade before noon, the bottom half of the door was also opened, meaning the bar was available, as well as lunch or supper fare. The saloon was divided into two sections. There was a plain plank bar, card tables, and chairs on one side, and two large tables with wooden bench seating on the other side for patrons to eat.

On the dining side of the saloon, a waist-high wall partly concealed a big stove and a Chinese cook with a single pigtail. The cook wore a black mud-treated silk suit, common to the Chinese.

The saloon was always busy serving food and drink to those who could pay and behave themselves until the Dutch door was shut top and bottom and locked and barred for the night.

We had one of the food tables to ourselves, and we had not delayed long waiting for the judge. The smell of stew bubbling on the stove and fresh baked biscuits from the oven had set our mouths to eating and savoring every delicious bite. Our meal with Judge Begbie would eventually become both a friendly send-off to our gold quest and a bit of a scrap. We had finished our meal before the judge arrived, full of words and good humor. Having settled on drinking first and eating later, Judge Begbie warned us that more gold hunters were moving beyond the Fraser Canyon. Word was that the nuggets had already been snatched up in the lower Fraser Canyon, and gold seekers were now intent on following the Fraser further and further north. Every river, creek, or stream emptying into the Fraser were being searched for gold. Miners and supplies for them were moving inland as never before. More ranches and farms were springing up to feed the endless gold seekers. The judge was excited about the developing British colony around him.

Jacque reminded him that the change brought by gold hunters was at the expense of the Native people who had been there long before even the Hudson's Bay Company. Claude listened quietly to all the conversations, but at Jacque's words to the judge, he added, "Change good for White men, bad for people here." The judge agreed that not all change was positive for everyone involved.

The judge, while drinking thirstily, wanted Henry Arden to suggest something to sing. Henry surprised us when he retrieved from a coat pocket, a case that turned out to hold a small flute when its parts were assembled. When Henry played the instrument, its beauty brought quiet to the saloon as the patrons listened to its clear, catchy, and lively tune, which Henry called a hornpipe. The judge was eager to share an operatic song that he loved. The lovely Violet, part owner with her brother of the Golden Nugget Saloon, offered to sing a song that was absolutely beautiful.

Mean Mike, drinking heavily to keep up to the judge, insisted on introducing Violet as his girl, and she was both charming and gracious to each of us. Claude's eyes lit up, and he could not help a grin that would not stop when Violet said to him, "You're too young and handsome to be stuck with these old fellas." When Violet left us to return to tending her bar, the judge looked at Mean Mike and said, "That beauty could make a man like you stop hunting gold and stay home."

Mean Mike was about to answer when Frenchy, an unwelcome rival from the past, accompanied by two of his brothers, yelled drunkenly from the saloon doorway, "Mike, have you any opium for me tonight? If you don't, I'll need to beat it out of you. How drunk are you?"

"Hardly drunk at all, so ye'd be left sober and sore. Buy us all a drink, if ye want to spend your money," Mike called to him.

"Hold it, Frenchy," Violet said, blocking the man from entering further into the tavern. "You know you're not welcome here. You cause fights and break up the place. Mike can come out to you, but you cannot come in here." Violet yelled to Mike, "If you want to meet up with Frenchy, go outside." Without a trace of fear in her voice, Violet then said to Frenchy, "My brother has his shotgun in his hands in case you and your brothers are thinking about coming in here, anyway."

In frustration and anger, Frenchy yelled at Violet, "Ta gueule, plouc, degage-toi."

Mean Mike rushed up to Frenchy and demanded, "What did ye say to her? Say it in English! You better not have insulted the lady! I'll teach you to talk to her with respect."

Frenchy just stared at Mike in drunken rage, his brothers looking eagerly for a fight behind him in the doorway.

Claude rushed up beside Mean Mike and said, "He says, 'Shut up, peasant, leave me alone.'"

Mean Mike looked at Claude and said in amazement, "How be ye know French, lad?"

"Everybody at the forts know insults and curse words in many languages," Claude answered.

"You shut up Mike and leave me alone. We don't want to drink here anyway," Frenchy said, turning as if to leave only to turn back and send a punch toward Mike. Quicker than usual, Mike avoided the fist, but Claude sprang at Frenchy, hammering two quick jabs to the side of the man's head, pushing him back into his brothers.

Frenchy's two brothers grabbed for Claude, but he was too quick and nimble. Claude brought the bottom of the door around and slammed it soundly into the three men. Mean Mike was so surprised, he just stood there watching Claude do all the fighting until the boy commanded, "You fight now, Mike!"

A pistol shot rang out above their heads, and the five of them at front door stopped in their tracks. The lovely Violet said with the authority of a deadly killer, "I will shoot anyone that moves. Frenchy, take your brothers and get out of here, now. Mike and Claude, go back and sit down before you break something, and learn to mind your own business. I don't need or want your help running this saloon." Frenchy and his brothers backed out the door, convinced Violet would shoot them if they didn't leave.

Mike and Claude rejoined us at the table, both stinging from Violet's scolding. Judge Begbie said it was great entertainment and Jacque, Henry, and me looked at each other in amazement. Mean Mike looked at Jacque and said, "Your lad would make any father proud."

The judge turned to Mike and said that the beautiful Violet would knock off his rough edges and have Mike drying the dishes in no time. Mean Mike smiled a drunk grin at the judge, bowed slightly, and said, "Shut up, peasant, and leave me the hell alone."

The judge roared in laughter and wanted to buy us another drink, but we declined because we needed to get back to our basecamp, as our gold hunt would be underway the next day. Henry, Jacque, and me all smiled as Claude helped an unsteady Mike reach the canoes. It was going to be an interesting journey with Claude along with us, as long as Mike didn't fall on him and crush the lad.

Back at camp, we sat around a fire, laying out plans for beginning our gold search. Last year, we had searched the gravel bars between Fort Hope and Yale and had done well. We had heard of rich gold bars further north in the Fraser Canyon beyond Yale. The question was, would it be a waste of time to search the same gravel bars again?

Claude spoke up, "Good to hunt in same place twice unless animals all gone. Must hunt to see if animals there. If there, hunt, if no there, move and hunt new place."

Mike drunkenly said, "I couldn't understand ye laddie, but that don't mean I don't like ye."

Henry Arden piped in, "In his own manner, he said that the only way to know if there is still gold to be found on the bars, is to look for it again. If there isn't any gold, we move on farther north."

"It seems like the thing to do," I added.

Jacque said, "Then let's start tomorrow at Murderer's Bar, for we are not far from it. We can search the area and leave our camp set up here. Put your hand up if you agree." Everyone voted with their hands, and it was unanimous, and we turned in for the night. It seemed like a short rest, but after black tea and a breakfast of fried rabbit, we were ready to push off for our gold hunting. Before heading out, Claude told us to call him CF on our travels, and he reminded us that the deer he had killed the day before needed to be smoked to save the meat. Mean Mike was badly hung-over and barely awake. He agreed to stay at the camp and begin smoking the deer meat, which would take a couple of days to complete. Mike was certainly strong enough to lift and hang and turn the quartered deer carcass in the smoke during the day.

We reached the Murderer's Bar and were surprised to see only six Chinese men working the far end. We did not try to pan for gold or set up our rocker near them. They ignored us, and we ignored them.

Henry and CF took to panning readily and found small traces of gold specks. Jacque and I worked the rocker with little results, so we switched places with our partners, and Henry and CF also enjoyed working the rocker. By early afternoon, Jacque and me were feeling disappointed, but our new partners were as eager as they had been from the start of the day.

Back from the bar about twenty-five feet, there was a small inlet with muddy flats leading to a gravel and sandy shore beside a rocky bank. CF asked if he could pan for gold in the small inlet, and Henry insisted on helping him. Jacque and me worked the rocker on the bar.

The water and mud in the inlet were about ankle deep. The mud, however, had great suction and was very slippery. After falls in the muck and laughter, our two partners made it to the shore and began panning for gold. Their shouts brought us to them after we also struggled in the wet muck and fell a few times. It was clear they had discovered a ridge that had some promising gold. We wanted more water to make panning and working our rocker more productive, so we needed a ditch to allow more water into the inlet and along the shore. We had a small spade, and we began trenching a small ditch. CF started in the river where the water was knee deep. Jacque stationed himself about three feet beyond CF, approaching the shore. CF trenched the river bottom toward Jacque. I was three feet in front of Jacque, and Henry was three feet in front of me. Each of us dug a trench three feet long to reach the next person. When CF had trenched his way to Jacque, he gave him the spade and moved beyond Jacque to be three feet in front of Henry. The three feet of moving soil and mud to dig the ditch was challenging, but it was a burst of work, and then a rest until it was your turn again. The trench had to keep going deeper toward the riverbank to encourage the water to flow right to the shore. Thankfully, the ditch only needed to be about fifteen feet long and about a foot wide.

When the trench was completed, we moved the rocker to the shore of the inlet. We were all wet and muddy, but we were also eager to pan and use the rocker until it was clear the sun was getting close to quitting for the day. Jacque offered to stay at our site. We were to bring him food and dry clothes and wood for a fire. We left him one canoe, and the three of us headed for basecamp as fast as our tired arms could move the oars.

CHAPTER FOUR:

A Muddy Search for Gold

WHEN WE ARRIVED at our basecamp, Mean Mike was surprised at our extremely muddy appearances but not at our excitement. He was always able to see the success of any venture. He was sure the ridge along the shore of the mudflat would cough up gold for us and eager to see the site and spend the night there with Jacque.

He had portions of deer meat ready for frying and a pot of baked beans ready. CF was eager to accompany Mike back to the gold site near Murderer's Bar. He was certain he could quickly return to us by canoe once he had dropped off food, wood, and clothes for his father. Mike grabbed supplies for himself, and then the two were heading back to the bar in short order. CF was paddling along with Mike, full of energy, as if he had been sleeping all day rather than working steadily. The canoe was not long vanishing downriver.

We had promised CF that we would wait to eat supper until he returned. The camp had the strong smell of cedar and pine wood from the smoking of the deer meat. Using canvas and trimmed tree limbs, Mike had made a three-sided enclosure to catch the smoke and channel it up to the hanging deer meat. The enclosure was as tall as Mike or six-feet five inches tall. He had the top covered with freshly cut pine branches and had gathered a good supply of green wood to add to the fire, which burned slowly, producing lots of extra smoke for the meat. We could see he had been busy and skillful about his task.

Henry, being a gentleman, was appalled at the mud he had collected on himself during the day. He was quick to get out of his dirty clothes and proceed to the river. There, he turned into a regular washer woman, attacking the mud on his garments as if it were a personal insult to him.

I decided his hatred of dirty duds could be supported, so I too was in the icy river with my long johns rolled up to my knees, scrubbing reluctant mud out of my clothes. I was no match for Henry, though. I quickly found a healthy aversion to the chilly water and became half-hearted about how clean my clothes needed to be. I hung my wet shirt and pants over a tree limb. Once I had changed into other garments, I placed the meat in a cast-iron frying pan so it would be ready for frying.

Henry finally came ashore with his washed clothes, and he also found a tree limb to hang them over. When Henry returned to the campfire in a clean outfit, he brought with him an iron for pressing clothes. He said, "Later, I'll heat the iron in the fire and iron my wet things dry."

I acted like ironing clothes was not out of the ordinary for me. Yet, I couldn't help saying to Henry, "You're welcome to also iron my clothes if you wish. I haven't had much practice at it."

"Hardly," Henry said, "I am not your butler. You may use my iron when I am done with my clothes. If you watch me, you'll learn how to do it quickly enough. Mind you, the iron is both hot and heavy, and it can give you a nasty burn if you don't keep your wits about you."

"I iron for you, Nothing," CF said, appearing again beside me like a ghost from nowhere. Henry and I both were startled.

Henry gasped, "Talk of the devil himself. CF, you startle a bloke coming upon him so quietly."

I blurted out, "You have to quit sneaking up on me, CF. It makes me want to yell. Don't do that! Let me see you or hear you before you get beside me. It's good to sneak up when hunting animals or enemies, but don't come up to friends like that."

"Not way of my people. We come up quietly to everyone. We hear friends and others say good and bad things. Want to hear what others saying when they not see us," CF explained.

"Just ask us, and we will tell you who and what we are talking about," Henry said to CF.

"Even if you talk bad of me?" CF asked.

"If we talk bad about you, we will say it to your face. You will know what we said and why. You can tell us if we are right or wrong about you," I explained to CF.

"Can I say ugly words about you to your faces?" CF asked.

"We would rather have you say them to our face than say them about us when we are not there to hear them," Henry answered honestly.

"I will not sneak up but will be Blue Jay when I come to you," CF said. "I iron clothes for Nothing, if he want."

"How do you know how to iron clothes?" I asked CF.

"White boss men at the fort demand their clothes and bedding be washed and ironed. I help grandmother and auntie do it. I do many things at the fort; I clean stables, split, and stack firewood, sweep floors, and work in gardens," CF answered me.

He might have said more but there was a flap of wings, and CF's crow landed on his shoulder and made a strange, muffled sound. In a hushed voice, CF said, "People sneaking up on us." CF and his crow moved out of sight, and Henry and I looked at each other and shrugged at the warning. I whispered to Henry, "We'll just act

31

like we don't know they are coming. We will look as if we're just preparing to eat." I put the cast-iron fry pan on the fire and casually said loud enough for our visitors to hear, "It won't take long to fry up this meat."

Henry followed my lead, putting his iron in the red coals of the fire. He whispered to me, "If you use a scorching skillet for defense, I'll need my hot iron." Then he said louder, for those sneaking up on us to hear, "I'm going for our plates while you are frying that meat."

"Hello, you've got company!" Frenchy emerged from the darkness with a stranger instead of a brother or two. His companion must have spoken, as Frenchy has a thick French accent. Frenchy looked strange. Usually a loud, brutish fellow, rough and ready to assert himself with a bodyguard of brothers, he seemed to be subdued and even a bit meek. Was he in shock, or afraid? I had no idea what to expect. The stranger said, "We hope you might show us some hospitality, and we promise to mind our manners."

"Frenchy, who is this that you are travelling with tonight? What do you want with us?" I asked our intruders.

The suit-dressed man with Frenchy said, "The name is Smith, and I am a Faro dealer. Frenchy and I are on our way to Yale. We are traveling lightly and could use a bit of food and shelter for the night."

Henry looked to me and said, "I think we could offer these men food and shelter, but you know Frenchy better than me."

"I agree we might," I stated, "but Frenchy, don't you have family you could stay with? Last year, you had lots of brothers with you when you were searching for gold with your group of about ten French men, at Murderer's Bar. You also had two brothers with you not long ago at the Golden Nugget Saloon. In fact, I have never seen you without them."

Frenchy answered me as if he was in daze, "I did have four brothers with me last year, but two were killed by Indians. I still have two brothers with me here. The other French men that were gold hunting with us have returned to France. My brothers and me cannot afford a passage home. Right now, they are at Hope." I had never seen Frenchy so subdued and quiet spoken before. He stood silently for a moment, then he seemed to come out of his somberness. He looked at Smith with pure hatred, then he looked at me and Henry with the same distaste.

Then red in the face with anger, he shouted at Henry and I, "I don't care a damn whether you help us or not. The only one of you any good for anything is Mean Mike, and he's a 'Tete de noeud.'" Looking at me, Frenchy pointed, then continued, "You petite, roi des cons. You tried to poison us last year."

Frenchy's loudness brought CF into the midst of the four of us, holding a rifle. CF remembered Frenchy from the Golden Nugget's front door and his fight with Frenchy and his brothers. Looking at Frenchy, CF asked, "Shoot this enemy?" He stood ready to fire, but he was waiting for an answer from Henry and me.

Frenchy snarled at CF, "Tell them what I called Mean Mike and this sawed-off runt. You told these ignorant English what I called the woman at the saloon."

"You want me to tell them before I shoot you?" CF said.

"You decide," muttered Frenchy. His anger and bluster seemed to be evaporating, and he was becoming quieter and more distraught again. It was my experience that Frenchy made the noise and stirred up trouble, expecting his brothers to do the fighting while he watched, so I did not think Frenchy was a threat since his brothers were not with him. He still had his bark, but he didn't have the bite of his brothers.

"He say Mean Mike, knot-head, and you, idiot. You want me to shoot him, Nothing? CF asked me.

"Maybe later," I said, laughing so that CF would know I did not feel we were in danger. "CF, put the rifle down. We don't shoot people, even Frenchy. Now, Mr. Smith, tell us why you have had the misfortune of traveling with Frenchy. Let's all sit down while you explain."

Mr. Smith said, "I am a Faro dealer at Hope. I met up with Frenchy and his brothers today. They wanted to play cards, and then they lost money at it. His two brothers tried to rush me and grab what was bet on the game. I shot them with my derringer. While his brothers were struggling with being wounded, Frenchy was trying to sneak up on me. I pointed my gun at him, and he backed off. Frenchy walked his brothers to the doctor, promising to get the constable after me." Mr. Smith paused and said to Frenchy, "Do you have anything to add to the story?"

Frenchy looked at Smith with hatred and said, "You'll be in hell before you know it!"

"Finish your story, Smith. Ignore Frenchy," I said.

Smith continued, "The owner of the saloon saw it all and knew that I acted in self-defense, but he doesn't want Frenchy and his brothers coming to get back at me. He said I couldn't continue to run my Faro game in his saloon, so I packed up my game and waited for Frenchy to arrive with the constable."

"Did the policeman ever show up with Frenchy?" Henry asked.

"No, only Frenchy returned, assuring me that the constable would be coming to arrest me. He said that the British judge will charge me with attempted murder, and he is called the hanging judge. Frenchy told me that his brothers will live, but I better leave Hope. I told him that I would shoot him if he didn't help me get away. Frenchy claimed that he has a saloon at Yale, where I can run my Faro game there until I find another establishment," Smith said in a tired and troubled voice.

I asked Frenchy if that was about the truth of it. Frenchy nodded his head yes in agreement. I looked at Smith, and I could only see a young man taking desperate action and following a path that would not end well. I knew from our experiences with Frenchy and his brothers last year that they were as dangerous as quicksand.

"Mr. Smith," I said, "It has been my experience that Frenchy cannot be trusted. While he may have a saloon at Yale, unless you kill his brothers, they will be after you as soon as they get the bullets out of their hides. I honestly think Frenchy will arrive there, but you probably won't.

I looked at Frenchy and said, "Sorry, Frenchy, to give you a bad character reference, but you were not counting on finding people who have had dealings with you and your brothers before. I wouldn't trust you as far as I could lift you, and that wouldn't be off the ground with your generous size."

There was definitely something wrong with Frenchy because what I said about him did not seem to offend or affect him one bit.

"I can take care of myself. I have already shot two men today," Smith said, seeming to assure himself of power he didn't feel.

"Is this the first time you have shot someone in a dispute over cards?" I asked him.

'Yes," he said in a tone that was full of regret.

"It's hard to face that you might have killed someone, I imagine," I continued.

"I felt threatened, but thank God, I did not kill either of them. I feel guilty as hell, though, even though I was defending myself. After I shot his brothers, I went out of the saloon and threw up. After hearing your words about Frenchy, should I really trust anything he says? I just wanted to get the hell out of there and not face the constable or anyone," Smith admitted.

"I would be willing to go back with you to Hope, as you tell the constable your side of things. It would be better to face it now, so it doesn't keep growing in power," I offered. I wanted to help Smith because I detected by his voice as he told his story that he was running on shock and panic. Shooting another person is traumatic. If I was wrong about all the trouble being with Frenchy and his brothers, they also needed to tell their side of the story to the constable. My support was with Smith, but gamblers are often great actors and manipulators of the truth.

Frenchy spoke up, "I think we should go back. Let the constable arrest him, then hang him."

Looking at me, Smith said, "I'd appreciate if you came with me. I need help thinking straight today."

"Let's go then. I'll follow you in our canoe," I replied. The truth was the way he said he needed help thinking straight made me wonder if he was not being honest about something.

"I will help Nothing row the canoe," CF offered.

Smith and Frenchy headed for their canoe, and we were only a minute or two behind them. We told Henry to eat supper, and we would eat when we got back to the camp or at the Golden Nugget.

Henry said, "Wait a minute, I'm coming with you in case you eat at the saloon. Besides, it's three musketeers, not two." Off we went feeling that we would be no more than an hour.

The canoe trip was short to Fort Hope, and we found the constable having a drink with Judge Begbie. Smith and Frenchy went and spoke with him, and I stood near Smith as he told his side of the story. The judge realized the men had an urgent matter with the constable, so he moved away from them and went and chatted with Henry and CF, his drink secure in his hand.

The owner of the saloon where Smith ran his Faro game had already told the constable that Frenchy's brothers had loudly complained that the dealer was cheating them, and they had tried to grab the dealer and his money. Smith had pulled out a pistol and shot them when they refused to stay back from him. Frenchy had been doing his best to move around and get behind Smith, and the owner had alerted the dealer of this. With Smith pointing his gun at Frenchy, the situation ended. The two brothers were shot but able to walk, and Frenchy helped them to the doctor's office. Each had a shoulder wound, and one had a bullet scratch on an ear. The other brother had a bullet crease on his side. The doctor had no trouble digging out the shoulder bullets, and the other two wounds were scratches. The wounded men were still resting at the doctor's office. There was little doubt they would be back to causing a disturbance in a short time.

The constable was not inclined to pursue any arrests or charges since he determined that it was a case of self-defense. Hearing the constable's verdict, Frenchy left to check on his brothers. The constable said to Smith that Frenchy and his siblings could be counted on to stir up trouble for him. Smith said he would keep that in mind, and he was relieved to have his dealing with the constable behind him. He offered to buy us a meal at The Golden Nugget, and we gladly accepted his offer.

The supper of the evening at the saloon was hash with slices of fresh baked bread. We introduced Violet and her brother to the Faro dealer, and we mentioned to Smith that Frenchy and his brothers were banned from The Golden Nugget. I asked Violet privately what she knew of the faro dealer, and she said, "He is handsome and charming, with the nature of a rattle snake." She didn't elaborate, and I didn't think we would see Smith again.

Bidding a farewell to Smith with full stomachs, we canoed back to our camp. We banked near the fire and added green wood to burn slowly in the night. Henry took his hot iron and pressed his clothes dry and free of wrinkles, while CF and I headed off to sleep like the dead.

The next morning, I discovered that Henry had also ironed my clothes. I tried to thank him, but he said, "Don't bother thanking me. Be assured it will never happen again."

I had awakened with the sunrise, feeling like my life was moving too fast for me to get enough sleep. We had fried deer meat and warmed up beans for breakfast, then headed to the gold site. Mean Mike and Jacque were working the rocker at the shore of the mudflat when we arrived. CF went back to our basecamp with Mike to help him make jerky from the deer meat, which Mike would continue smoking again—it was ideal to chew when we were panning gold.

CF knew how his people made jerky. The secret was to cut very thin pieces or strips of meat, pound it as flat as possible, then lay the beaten-out segments to dry on rocks or hang them in the direct sunlight. The pieces on rocks needed to be turned over every hour. The sun and wind would dry the wet thin strips of meat quickly, and if the meat still refused to dry, it could be fried quickly on each side to do it further. After the meat had dried, it would be smoked to ensure it could be kept and eaten for many days.

CF returned to our gold site by noon.

Like the day before, the Chinese were continuing their search for gold on Murderer's Bar, near our inlet site. The Chinese tended not to keep a canoe near them when working several days at a gold site.

Somewhere close by, they would have a tiny camp, where they would retreat to and from on foot. The Fraser River was acting unpredictable at the site, which was its nature. Our work of digging a trench through the mudflat yesterday was rendered unnecessary today. The level of the river had changed overnight, and it had covered the mudflat with knee deep water. Panning and working with the rocker proved successful. The amount of gold we found increased gradually during the day. We were in good spirits at having an early taste of success.

We did notice, however, that the water level in the mudflat kept rising over the course of the day. The current of the river became faster as the day progressed. Upstream there must have been a heavy rain or snow cover melt in the high mountain peaks because the river was becoming more swollen and aggressive. It had picked up both speed and force, warning that it was willing to carry off anything in its way. As we focused on finding gold, we heard yelling coming from the Chinese working on Murderer's Bar. One of the men in their group had been swept into the river and was being carried away by the fast, powerful current. CF, Jacque, and Henry tossed me their gold pans and headed for our canoe. I caught their pans as I was working the rocker, and I watched them jump in and seek to guide the canoe into the river, around the bar and in the direction of the struggling man caught by the powerful current.

I couldn't see from the inlet if our canoe was able to reach the Chinese man in time. I waited for my partners to return, while anxiously pulling the handle of the rocker. After an eternity, our canoe pulled up on the far side of the bar, and a Chinese man was helped out. His group surrounded him and bowed in thanks to the men in our canoe. My partners soon returned to the inlet, looking pleased with themselves. I congratulated them on a well-done rescue effort. CF said, "Why have they no canoe of their own?"

Jacque replied, "They don't need one when we're around." Henry and I laughed aloud when CF rolled his eyes and shook his head at his father's answer to his question.

Because the river was high and flowing rapidly, we decided to take the rocker and go home in the late afternoon. The trip to our basecamp was not far, but it was hard rowing because we were going against the powerful current.

When we reached camp, Mean Mike came to greet us as we beached the canoes. "We have two visitors, and one is the constable," Mike informed us with a silly grin. "Watch yourself, lads, I don't want any of you gettin' arrested." Mike was enjoying himself, and we were at a loss as to what fun he was having at our expense.

CF touched Mike's arm and said, "If you fight constable, I not help you." Henry, Jacque, and I all joined in, "Me neither!"

Mike laughed and led us to our guests. The constable nodded to us and said to me directly, "I know you were with the Faro dealer last night, and I have him with me today. Word is that Frenchy and his brothers are boasting that they are going to kill him. I cannot force Smith to leave Hope, but I suggested—at the advice of Matthew Begbie—that he travel on further up the Fraser in your company. Would you men allow him to do so?" he asked as he looked at each of the five of us.

The constable could see our surprise and reluctance, so he said, "I have him waiting out of sight, as it is better if he doesn't hear you say that you don't want him to travel with you. I can't obligate you or him to journey together; I am merely trying to prevent a murder."

Mean Mike spoke up eagerly, "I'm for it, as he can teach us all about Faro, so I can win at it instead of losing."

Jacque said after Mike, "I have no problem, but only if he is searching for gold in the mud like the rest of us. He can play cards at night after he has worked as hard as we do."

Henry was next, "I agree with Jacque. This is a partnership of gold seekers, if he is willing to hunt gold with us, he can travel with us until he wants to leave."

CF said after Henry, "I'm okay if him want come."

Lastly, I said, "Constable, go tell Smith it is okay if he comes along, but he must be willing to hunt gold with us. He won't be dealing Faro while he is with us except at night when the work is done."

The constable brought the dealer in and told him the conditions for traveling with us. Smith said it was to his advantage to not be seen as a Faro dealer but a miner for a while. He would work with us at least to Yale.

We invited the constable to join us for supper but a meal with us didn't seem to enthuse him, and he left us with Smith, who had brought a few personal belongings with him.

Mean Mike, Jacque, and I thought this time we had a young man Magee named Smith. You had to have been with us the first time around for it to make sense, but it did to us.

CHAPTER FIVE:
One Man Too Many

SMITH WOULD PROVE six men are too many for a partnership. From the first night of his travels with us, he broke our group in two, by that I mean three against three. Mean Mike, having been at the camp all day, had cooked a pot of deer stew for our supper. Right off, we divided over eating the stew right away or waiting a while, giving some a chance to clean up first. Smith, Henry, and Jacque wanted to eat a bit later, and Mike, myself, and CF wanted to eat right away.

Smith offered to flip a coin to settle the question. Mean Mike objected to him tossing the coin because he felt gamblers could not be trusted. Smith's face remained calm at Mike's words, but Henry quickly told him that Mike said stuff without thinking. Henry suggested that the youngest person among us flip the coin.

Sometimes the simplest question takes on exaggerated importance and far too much time to answer. CF agreed to toss the coin in the air, if it landed heads up, we ate right away, if it was tails, we waited. CF tossed the coin a nice height in the air, and his pet crow flew in and caught it in its beak and flew off with it.

Three of us laughed and thought the crow catching the coin was funny. Three were annoyed and frustrated that the coin had to be tossed again. CF quickly tracked down his bird and brought the coin back. Mean Mike announced that he would toss the damn coin and have it done with this time. He snatched the coin out of CF's hand and threw it in the air. The crow flew for the coin again, flapping its wings in front of Mike's face. The bird flying so close caused Mike to jump and yell, "What the hell!?" He threw up his arms in defense. His one arm hit the coin, which went flying through the air. It made a loud clang on the edge of the pot and disappeared into the stew.

Three men saw the coin hit the stew pot and dive in. Three didn't believe it. The only thing to be done was to eat the stew to prove whether the coin was in the pot or not. The six of us were divided as we ate our first meal together as a new group, and it was the start of things to come. Mean Mike was adamant that the coin was not in the stew. He would not heed the advice to be careful and not chip a tooth on the coin or choke on it. When Mike let out a yell because he had bitten hard on the coin, five out of six of us were smiling.

I felt sorry for Smith the next morning, as at sunrise he was prodded awake and given strong black tea to drink. He turned his nose up at porridge for breakfast until he realized it was that or nothing. He was off with us to search for gold in a plain shirt, corduroy trousers, and questionable shoes. Because two of us worked on the rocker at a time, he could use someone's gold pan. CF stayed in our basecamp to continue the smoking of the deer meat, and he hoped to catch fish for a change of food. He offered to make us bannocks, which would be a treat from biscuits or sourdough bread.

Bannock was a staple food of Scottish fur traders and became part of the life of Indigenous people as well. CF made a dough of flour, bacon fat, salt, and water into fry bread, which was a flat-round cake or pancake. Often his fry bread was flavored with honey, berries, or natural herbs that he found at hand. His bannocks were a delight to eat.

It was Smith who first found gold in his pan. When he realized that all the gold, we found was held by Jacque to be divided evenly between us later, he was appalled. He managed to adjust to the reality of it during the day when others found gold that went to Jacque, and he hadn't found any more himself.

Our light lunch was a standard feast of stale crackers, dry bread crusts, or some dried apple slices. When we rested for a break, Smith fell asleep, having put forth a good effort all morning—a fact on which everyone agreed. When Smith awoke from a short nap and we were ready to return to work, Mike handed him his hat. Mike saw that Smith was already badly sunburned on his face and neck. Mean Mike said that we would take turns sharing our hats with Smith, as we were accustomed to being outside, but Smith was not. Jacque and CF did not wear hats and did not burn and blister in the sun, but the rest of us needed hats to face the sun and extremes of weather. Smith was thankful for the opportunity to have a hat to shade his sunburn.

Early afternoon proved to be productive for us, as tiny amounts of gold kept appearing steadily in our pans and our rocker. It was a steady supply of tiny particles, but our spirits were high for some days, there might not even be a hint of gold. We were thankful for any success we found.

Henry began to sing; and I was familiar with the song and joined in. Henry and I were pleased when Smith sang along, and we were delighted when Mean Mike also added his excellent tenor voice. We pressured Jacque into joining too. He had been reluctant because he said that he had a deep singing voice. Henry explained to Jacque that a deep voice, called a bass voice, was a special talent for he was able to sing from second E below middle C to the E above middle C. Jacque and everyone except Henry, himself, were clueless about the below and above C and E stuff, but Henry impressed us all with his words. Henry coached Jacque through the song when we sang it again. The third time through, we all sang loudly and confidently, causing the Chinese men to clap from the place at the end of Murderer's Bar. It was a rare feel-good moment for all of us.

As the afternoon wore on, we had a burst of excitement when we found an abundant amount of gold. When we had our hopes up that we would keep discovering more, it vanished without any trace. In frustration, Mike pulled out his flask of whiskey and had two drinks. He asked, "Anyone else want a drink?"

Henry answered, "Thanks for the offer, Mike. Maybe later."

Jacque said, "Pass it over, I could use one."

Smith spoke up with a grin on his face, "I'm not used to all this physical work and fresh air. A drink of whiskey would put this aching body of mine to sleep. You guys would just leave me here in the mud.

I'll just keep trying to stay awake and live long enough to finish this first day."

Smith didn't know it, but he had already gained our respect, as he had worked at the rocker and the gold panning as hard as anyone. It was obvious he was competitive and wanted to keep up with us, or maybe even work harder than us. Searching for gold was pure, hard work, often without any reward for our effort. It was no small task to keep at it steadily hour after hour.

I said to Mike, "You know I throw up if I drink beer. No one here wants me to drink whiskey and vomit."

"I'll put my flask away then," Mike said, "No use wastin' good whiskey."

We worked until near sunset, and Smith asked us what the odds were of finding more gold here at the mudflat, as we must have worked them out. Jacque said it usually came down to moving on when we had decided we had been at a spot long enough and that it was time to move on.

Smith asked, "We haven't found a trace of gold in the last three hours. It seems to me that we have panned across the shore of this ridge, and we have covered samples of earth from the ridge itself extensively. Is it time to move upriver? What are the chances of finding more gold if we come back tomorrow?"

Henry spoke up, "That a good question. If we come back tomorrow, will we just be beating a dead horse?"

"What's a dead horse have to do with anything?" Mike asked, at a loss.

"It's just a way of saying would it be wasting our time searching for more gold here if there isn't any," I explained.

Jacque said, "So is the horse dead, or isn't it? I'm not convinced it's dead. Everybody think about it, and we'll take the rocker with us. We'll discuss it and vote on it tonight after supper."

Smith asked, "Couldn't we just vote on it here and now?"

I said, "We make our plans together, and everyone gets a vote. CF is not here to vote."

Smith said, "It'll wait till later then."

Mike was frustrated with the crazy talk of dead horses and took another two gulps of whiskey to drown his rising temper. We canoed back to camp, muddy and challenged by Smith to be strategic about our gold hunting. The odds of finding more were not stacked in our favor, as we were going where other gold seekers had gone before us. We would be picking up what they missed. Were we ready to move on to unexplored areas?

When we arrived at camp, CF had fish fillets ready for frying and a good number of bannocks prepared. He had one potato for each of us, roasting in the coals. Those who wanted to clean up before eating headed to the river. Most of us just grabbed our plates and waited to get a piece of hot fish to accompany our potato and bannocks. Henry and Smith ate last, their hands washed and muddy clothes soaking in river water for a final scrubbing after supper. They didn't bother changing and ate their supper in their long johns. Jacque said we would discuss and vote on moving upriver after everyone had time to relax and those scrubbing their clothes were finished. We were surprised to see CF talking in his native tongue for a considerable amount of time with Jacque, but we minded our own businesses.

It was almost dark as we sat on dead tree limbs that we had pulled up around the campfire. We had two campfire areas set up: one with a three-sided enclosure for smoking meat, and then an open one for cooking, light, and a bit of heat, as the evenings were both damp and cool by the river. Before Jacque got to the discussion, I thanked CF for catching, cleaning, and frying fish and great tasting bannocks. The others all praised CF for supper.

Jacque said, "Before we discuss staying or going upriver, CF tells me we had visitors here at camp this afternoon. He was up the bank in the forest, gathering wood, when his crow gave him warning of visitors. Watching from the bushes of the upper bank, he saw Frenchy and two other men snooping around the camp."

With one of his silly grins, Mike said, "That Frenchy can't live without us! Poor lad can't take rejection. He's acting as stubborn as a Scotsman."

"He is like an itch that you can't reach to scratch. We should give him the money to go home to France," I said.

"Would we have to pay for his brothers too?" Henry questioned.

Jacque spoke up to get us back to his son's story. "CF said that he brought his bow and arrow with him, hoping to shoot a rabbit as he gathered wood. So, he got his bow and arrow ready and kept watching the men below as they poked around our camp. Frenchy bent over and stuck his head in one of the tents. It was a big easy target for CF, who shot an arrow that struck Frenchy in his seat!"

Jacque had to pause in telling us CF's story again because there was a loud applause from us.

"There's more," Jacque said with satisfaction in his voice. "Frenchy howled and screamed, 'Get it out!' One of the men with him ran for their canoe, the other yanked the arrow from Frenchy's behind. Another arrow from CF pierced the man's hat. He pulled the hat off his head, looked at the arrow in his hat, dropped it, and ran for their canoe. Frenchy staggered after them, and they helped him into the boat. They paddled away, but CF sent one more arrow that stuck in the side of their canoe. They disappeared, yelling French curses to the air."

Smith spoke up and questioned in a serious tone, "Did the two men with Frenchy seem to have wounded shoulders?"

Jacque looked to CF and said something in their native tongue, and CF shook his head no in reply. Jacque commented that Frenchy probably brought a couple of friends with him.

Mike said, "Frenchy don't have any friends just brothers."

I suggested that we take turns guarding the camp during the night in case they came back to get even with us. Henry felt that they might have been looking to see if they could see any sign that Smith was with us.

Once again, we all praised CF for chasing away our uninvited snoopers with his bow and arrow.

Jacque asked, "Who wants to take turns guarding the camp during the night? Put your hand up if you do." Three wanted a guard, and three did not. Jacque said, "I will flip a coin. If it is heads, we have guards. CF does your crow fly at night?" When CF shook his head no, Jacque flipped a coin and the coin dictated that there would be no guards during the night.

He continued, "If you think we should leave the mudflat and move upriver, speak for it or against it, and then we will vote."

I spoke first, "I suggest Henry and me spend the morning taking one last look for gold at the mudflats with just our gold pans. We can also check closer toward the Chinese men on the bar. I also recommend that Jacque, CF, and Smith go exploring upriver for the next

RAYMOND MAHER

gravel bar or a creek emptying into the Fraser that we could search for signs of gold. Mike could stay at camp and smoke the meat. We can all return by noon and decide where we might go or if we think it would be wise to stay longer. If we choose to go upriver, we can all help take down the camp quickly."

Mean Mike responded to my suggestions, "I'll try and get lots of smoke going for the meat in the morning."

"I would be glad to go with Nothing to see if we can spot any signs of gold," Henry offered.

CF announced, "I go with father and Smith."

Smith declared, "I'm in agreement with everything."

Jacque commanded, "Put your hand up if you agree with our plans for tomorrow?" All hands were in favor.

We were all tired and off to bed in our tents shortly after the vote on the next day's plans. At sunrise, Jacque, CF, and Smith were off upriver, searching where we might head next. Their canoe was a dot on the river when Henry and I were rising. We departed for the mudflats shortly after them, leaving Mike banking the campfire with green wood to get as much smoke as possible on the deer meat.

When we arrived at the mudflats, Frenchy's two brothers were waiting for us. They informed us that they were looking for the Faro dealer. They could see he wasn't with us. I could say I hadn't seen him when they asked because I hadn't actually seen him that morning. I told the brothers that Smith wasn't at our camp, and they could go there and see for themselves. The brothers indicated that they would do that next.

When they were gone, Henry asked me if Mike would be all right. I said, "Mike was hardly civil to us this morning. Early morning is his grouchy time. Worry about the brothers, as it's been a while since Mike has been in a brawl."

The morning passed quickly because we tried various places to see if there was gold we had missed. We even looked along Murderer's Bar next to the Chinese men, without any measurable success, so we returned to basecamp a little before noon.

When we arrived at camp, we could not see Mean Mike. I was feeling really guilty when we couldn't immediately locate him. What if Frenchy's brothers had harmed him? I sure hoped they hadn't hit Mike on the head because of his history of suffering from concussion. I was genuinely relieved to find Mike asleep in a drunken slumber by the fire. He had his empty whiskey flask beside him. "We'll let him sleep until the others return," I told Henry.

In his stash of supplies, Henry had coffee. He offered to make a big pot that we could all share and it would help sober Mike up. The strong smell of fresh coffee greeted Jacque, CF, and Smith when they came into camp.

We roused Mike from his sleep and gave him a cup of coffee to help him sober up. He shared that Frenchy's brothers had stopped at our camp and were satisfied that Smith wasn't with him. He offered them a drink from his flask, but they had their own, and they all had a couple of drinks together before they left, satisfied the Faro dealer wasn't with us. After Frenchy's brothers were gone, Mike found his flask couldn't stay away from his lips—until he had drunk it dry. We accepted his story as most likely accurate, and we all enjoyed a cup of coffee with him, even Jacque.

We shared that we couldn't find any more promising traces of gold at the mudflats or Murderer's Bar. Jacque, CF, and Smith had found another bar and a creek emptying into the Fraser that we could search on our way up the river. They had a spot picked out beside the creek for our camp, which was also near the next gravel bar.

CHAPTER SIX:
Moving on and Going Strong

IT DID NOT take long for us to pack up and move upriver. The spot for our new camp was beside the mouth of a creek that we hoped to search for gold. The creek was wide and deep, so it needed to be explored by canoe. We wondered if anyone else was looking for gold along its banks? Jacque and his two partners reported that the gravel bar in the Fraser River had both White and Chinese prospectors.

We decided that we would get our camp set up first, then secure firewood for the night. Next, we would check out the bar in the Fraser to see if there was space for us to look for gold there, as it might have claims filed on it. After that, we needed to explore the creek for any prospectors, as well as gold promising gravel bars.

There was a sense of excitement in finding out what we wanted to know. Mean Mike, Jacque, and Henry were the right partners for approaching the Fraser River gravel bar. Jacque often knew people from working at Hudson's Bay Company forts, which made getting information easier. Mean Mike was a giant of a man, respected for his size and strength, and he gave a presence of authority to their group. Henry had a confident manner without giving offense, a gracious disarming smile, and an open respect for anyone he met. Mike was the wild card in the mix. As long as he allowed the other two men to do the talking, things would remain positive.

In the meantime, Smith, CF, and I explored the creek. Although CF was the youngest of the three of us, he was the most experienced with navigating a canoe, and he set ours on course, upriver. Rowing against the creek current was easier than the Fraser's current. The creek, flowing deep and wide, followed a mostly straight line north eastward. After about three miles, it made a long s-shaped curve before continuing to directly flow in a straight northeastward course again.

We decided to explore the s-curve of the river which had a number of gravel ridges along it, as well as shallows and small fingers of water trapped in the overflow areas of the creek. We beached the canoe and armed with our gold pans, began panning to see if there might be any traces of gold.

Excited and engrossed in our task, time lost its meaning. It was CF who alerted us to the truth that the sun had set, and we needed to head for camp or stay there all night. The trip back was easy rowing with the current. The three of us were excited because we had each found gold. The s-curve of the creek was well worth checking out again. When we reached camp, the others had already returned from the bar on the Fraser. Jacque was ready to fry bacon and potatoes for supper and enlisted CF to prepare bannocks. It was dark by the time supper was over, and we lingered around the campfire, each group sharing the day's report.

The group from the Fraser bar reported that all the spaces in the area were already claimed and looking for gold there wasn't possible at this time. The good thing was a miner there wanted meat for his men and asked if he could buy or trade with us if we had extra meat. He had potatoes, rice, tea, and flour to exchange.

Henry had negotiated a trade deal with the man. When they had returned to camp, he and Mean Mike had taken a portion of deer meat back to the bar and brought back the goods. They were pleased to hear that we had found gold and that there was a chance there might be more on the bend of the creek we had explored. We would all return to the creek the next day to gather any gold we could find.

There was one other order of business. We needed to take turns staying at camp one day at time. The person staying must hunt meat or fish and prepare the breakfast and supper. They were also responsible for finding firewood and watching the camp against thieves. Visitors would become more numerous as we worked our way toward Fort Yale and beyond. Both Smith and Henry were alarmed at the thought of cooking. They joked that they would only need to cook once or twice to be relieved of camp duty. Three of us remembered the excellent camp master we had in Old Man Magee, who made our lives comfortable and fed us with good vitals. With the exception of CF, none of us this second time around was much good at cooking.

Mean Mike wanted Smith to tell us about the game of Faro before we separated for the night.

Smith said to us, "You realize, gentlemen, that professional gamblers like me, come in every shape, size, age, background, skill level, and degree of honesty. Some of the best professional gamblers are ladies," Smith said with a smile.

He then said, "Playing cards has always been a major source of entertainment. When people bet, even a small win is intoxicating. A big win is a personal glory. Faro is so popular because it is one of the simplest gambling games ever devised. It is said to have come from France, with the first French cards having a picture of an Egyptian Pharaoh on their back."

Smith paused, then continued, "Today, Faro is not in its simplest form. Each turn, players bet against the house, placing their money or token upon a green cloth with painted images of thirteen cards, ace through king. Usually, spades are shown on the cloth, but their suit doesn't matter. Only the card's face value is counted. The dealer then deals two cards from a standard deck. The players want to predict which cards will be turned over next. The first card revealed in each turn is the losing bet. The bank collects those. The second card is a winning bet. The bank pays those out. If a pair of cards is revealed, the house takes half of any bet on that card; it's called a split."

Smith stopped for a second to confirm how much we knew about the game and to see if any of us had ever played it. Only CF and I had not, however, we had both watched it being played.

Smith asked those who had played, what they had liked about it. The positive opinions were that it was a fast-action game, with easy-to-learn rules, and it offered better odds than most games of chance.

In our group, poker was considered slow, but it was often the game of people who could afford to bet big and lose big. Faro was any and every man's game.

A single dealer or banker often ran Faro in frontier places. By banker, it meant that Smith was the one overseeing the bets, paying the winners and collecting from the losers on each set of two cards revealed. He handled the money. If Smith was running the game at a saloon, he would give a percentage of his earnings to the saloon owner.

Smith admitted that he considered himself a small business-man, managing money and having financial dealings with people like a banker. He always dressed in a dark suit to fit the image of a professional.

As a group, we agreed with Smith that gambling was considered a profitable and respectable way of making a living unless the gambler gained a reputation for being dishonest or a killer in disputes about the game.

None of us disputed Smith's view that gamblers, lawyers, and bankers were both respected and mistrusted. Smith had considered becoming a lawyer because he was fixated on winning and competing. He prized himself on outwitting others in any situation. He could see himself arguing cases in court, but he could not see himself enduring years of study or reading endless law books. His handlings of his parents, siblings, teachers, neighbors, friends, and enemies were calculated strategies to be the winner. Gambling fit his need to experience the adrenalin rush of playing the odds. He liked the gut-jarring, win-or-lose life of a gambler.

If we could have looked into Smith's hidden side, we would have seen that he was an actor. He could be all things to all people to win their confidence. Not exactly a full con artist but very much an imposter, and always a very believable fellow, able to fool others. He was a loner, impressed with himself as a professional gambler, and building a tidy profit at the expense of others. He liked to think of himself as a lone shark, hungry for suckers and their shed blood here and there. Presently, he viewed being a Faro dealer as a steppingstone to being a gambler in the bigger profit poker games.

As Smith was talking, Mean Mike asked him at least three times to share with us some helpful tips to win at Faro. The third time, Smith said, "Mike, what is key in Faro and all card games, is remembering every card that has been played so that can make wise bets in that knowledge. It would seem you don't have to remember suits in Faro, but the winning edge comes with knowing what has been played. The better you remember as the game progresses, the more money you can make with later bets."

"Let me show you what I mean," he continued, pulling out a deck of cards. "Most players focus on the winning card or cards, but every card turned over is important, as each one tells you what is still left in the dealer's hand."

Focusing on all of us, Smith said, "Let's make it interesting. I will turn over two cards, ten times. See, here to begin with, I have turned over the five of hearts and now the seven of clubs. I will then turn over two more cards and place them onto the two I turned over first. This time it is an ace of clubs, and now a nine of spades. Now I will pick these cards up, put them back in the deck, and reshuffle again."

Having finished shuffling, Smith announced, "Now, ten times I will turn over two cards, face up. Each time I turn up two new cards, they will cover up the two turned over before. After ten turns of exposing two cards each time, you will have seen twenty cards turned over. Then I will ask you to tell me the twenty cards you have seen. I will do it fairly slowly, so you can all see the two cards each time. Anyone think they can remember the twenty cards?"

Mean Mike said, "Only if I was drunk."

"Never wise to gamble drunk, "Smith said dryly.

"How many gamble drunk?" Mike asked.

"Too many," Smith said, then quickly asked Mike, "Do you think you could remember the first four or six pairs I turn over?"

I'll try," he said.

"That leaves ten or twelve cards for the rest of you to remember. I will give the rest of you a chance to consider how you can remember the other ten or twelve cards between you or will you each try to remember the pairs Mike cannot remember. I will allow you to signal each other for ten seconds, but no words or whispering." Smith closed his eyes and counted aloud, "10,9,8,7,6,5,4,3,2,1. Time is up."

Everyone was up for the challenge, and it was as quiet as a grave as we watched Smith turn over two sets of cards ten times. "Gentlemen," he said, "The last two are face up, so everyone should be able to name them. Mike, tell me, of the eighteen cards that are left, how many pairs do you remember as being turned over?"

Mike started confidently; "The jack of spades and the eight of diamonds, the three of clubs and the nine of hearts, the two of clubs and the ace of diamonds, the six of clubs and the six of hearts, and that's it—I'm done, it's all I can remember."

"Good job, Mike," Smith said, honestly impressed, "Who remembers the other ten cards that were turned over?"

I said, "The seven, queen, and eight of hearts."

Henry said, "The five of clubs, seven of clubs, and the king of clubs."

Jacque said, "Three of diamonds, and queen of diamonds."

CF said, "Ace of Spades, queen of spades."

"Gentlemen let's expose the cards and make sure it is an honest identification," Smith said, picking up the eighteen cards in his hand. He did not pick up the last two he had turned over. He said to Mike, "You memorized the cards as pairs as they were turned over. Remembering four pairs was excellent." Smith dealt out of the eighteen cards in his hand, the eight cards Mike had named.

Smith turned to me and said, "Nothing, it seems you memorized hearts." He dealt to me the hearts I had named.

"Henry, you memorized clubs correctly," Smith said as he dealt Henry the clubs he had named.

Smith continued, "Jacque and CF, you had the diamonds and spades covered." He dealt them the cards they had named, and then all the cards in his hand were gone.

Smith said, "I have used this test many times before to show that people often play Faro leaving everything to luck. I have never had an individual or group able to name all the cards turned over until tonight. How did you signal what suits you each were to remember?"

I answered, "We each made the obvious signs like a hand on the heart, pointing to a finger, a clubbing or spading motion."

"In most groups, they try to remember all the pairs on their own," Smith said, caught off guard at our success.

After silence and head shaking, Smith said, "Really Impressive! Most have no idea what to do during the count of ten. I may have met my match in competing with you. Here are further things to ponder. How many threes were turned up by the tenth turn, in the first ten hands? How many queens? If four of each were turned up, you would be able to bet wisely in placing your bets on the cloth."

We acknowledged our thanks to Smith, as his tips could be helpful for us. Mike was looking forward to the next time he played Faro and winning at it. We wondered if he could play sober enough to remember the cards played each turn.

It was an interesting interaction, and we all went to bed pleased for the diversion from our daily gold searching.

CHAPTER SEVEN:
Suffering a Heart Attack from Greed

OUR HOPES WERE high that the long s-curve of the creek might offer us gold in our pans and rocker. We went up the creek the next morning to assess the gravel ridges on its long curve. We worked morning to night for seven days, gathering a good showing of gold. The eighth day, even we three seasoned gold hunters gave in to daydreaming about our expanding wealth because of the discovery of a dozen gold nuggets of splendid size.

We all noticed that Smith's face lit up with open idolization of the gold nuggets that we found. At first, we accepted it as the excitement of a new experience for him. In time, though, it became an irritation, as Smith became more bedeviled with whatever gold we discovered. When anyone gave gold to Jacque to hold, Smith had to see its amount and value. It also became clearer that he still resented that all the nuggets were held by Jacque to be split evenly among the six of us. He did not say anything, but he could not hide from us his appetite for the gold we found. It wasn't enough for Smith to find gold, he wanted to hang on to it. With our present success, it was disappointing to see gold becoming an obsession for the Faro dealer. By the tenth day, to Smith's disappointment, the gold began to play out, and it seemed like we would need to move before long to a new location on the creek or return to the Fraser and continue our search.

Also on the tenth day, seven men came down the creek and stopped to talk with us. They had followed the creek upstream until it disappeared into high mountain waterfalls. There were two gold prospectors in their group who were searching for veins of gold that would need more labor to extract. They wanted to grab surface nuggets but were also intent on more serious mining.

Smith was impressed with the two men, who claimed to know about rocks and the potential of mining below the surface of the ground. They alleged that they were educated in geology and trained in mining. The group asked if they could look for gold on the creek curve, as well as ourselves. Since we had covered all of the curve except the farthest north end, we told them that they were welcome to set up camp at the south end. As we worked at the north end of the curve, there would be a reasonable distance between us.

When we returned to camp, Mike had a big pot of rabbit stew ready, which he dished out to us for supper. Smith and I were the last ones served, and we sat close on a log separate from the others. I challenged Smith as we ate, "You've had a keen interest in the gold we have found the last couple of days."

Between mouthfuls, Smith admitted, "When we found those nuggets, I could hardly keep my hands off them or keep my eyes in my head. They brought out every greedy emotion in me. I actually wanted to continue gold hunting much longer when I saw them. I thought if I did keep going, I must stack more odds in my favor. Not to offend you, but I find your group is too relaxed, not focused enough on getting rich. I also realized that you lack any experts on mining and geology. I did go a little insane with greed at the finding of those nuggets. I believe I have regained my sanity, though, at least until we find nuggets like that again."

"Smith," I said to him, "Sanity is only ever a temporary condition. It is a wise man who recognizes his insanities. My craziness is my temper and my desire to doctor people in their bodies and souls. I cannot make up my mind if I am insane enough to become a surgeon. Smith, I believe you don't like being here with us. Still, I think you have done a remarkable job of hiding your distaste of us."

Smith let his guard down and was honest with me. He blurted out, "From the first night you accepted me at the constable's request, I have wanted to escape. I respect every one of you, but I have always been a loner. I've considered my time traveling with you just slightly better than doing jail time. Your partnership strangles my need to be in charge. I find it frustrating to co-operate with everyone by voting on decisions. I hate that the gold found is shared equally. I see myself living and dying by competing with and getting the better of others. Just being the same as everyone else goes against my grain. I need to be ahead. I don't want to be a friend or a partner to anyone."

"I assumed as much," I said, "But you have been respectful of us as a group and as individuals. There is nothing wrong with wanting to be independent and do things the way you desire. I think that few can be as autonomous as they want or achieve getting rich without the help of others. I hope if you ever find yourself helpless and in need of a friend, you'll consider asking God to partner up with you."

"Nothing," Smith said to me, "I know you and Henry are into God, the Bible, and prayer, and I appreciate you have respected my choice to ignore all three. My ignoring them isn't likely to change. The way I see it, friends, or partners or even God could only get in the way of my ambitions to be a rich gambler. I have no desire to be poor or average or concerned about others. I have my mind set on playing my life my way."

"Smith," I offered, "You may well stay a loner and become a wealthy gambler. As I see it, the hitch is that wealth, whether it's gold or money, does not have any loyalty to its owners. If you are shot in a dispute about cards, your money will go with your killer. If they put your money and gold in your coffin, you won't have any fun spending it there."

Smith registered an offended look at hearing my words and did not say anything. He looked at me in the eye like I had just said something more stupid than ridiculous nonsense.

"Sorry," I said, "That was a sermon you didn't ask to hear. Ignore what I said to you. I try not to express my opinions unless they are invited, but as you just experienced, I can overstep other people's boundaries."

"Nothing," Smith said with a fake smile like he was talking to a small, clueless child, "I won't bother to dispute the logic of your words which puts my desire for wealth in a questionable light. Money or gold make being alive truly inviting. I prefer to become as rich as I can for as long as I can."

Before Smith and I could talk more, a sudden wind came upon us, ushering in heavy rain. We all quickly sought the shelter of our two tents. Each tent could accommodate three men. These were our refuge from the weather, the night, the cold and dampness, and the overwhelming sense of being intruders in the wilderness. The wind gusts shook the tents, and the heavy rain hammered our canvas walls, as if we might dare to forget their presence. Both the rain and wind refused to quiet down all evening and were ready to abuse any of us who dared to leave our tents. Morning gave little let up in the heavy rain, but the wind had left us to stir things up somewhere else.

Our tent was the meeting place for the six of us in the morning. Together we proclaimed it a Sunday, a day of rest, a free day. Our occasional 'Sundays' were reserved for really nasty weather days. One tent was for anyone who wanted to get extra rest, and the other was a place for relaxing talk, cards, checkers, reading, or other leisure activities. These were also fasting days until the rain or storm let up enough to have a campfire and cook some food. We fasted on our stashes of crackers, jerky, dried fruit, and the like.

The rain stopped mid-afternoon, and the sun broke through the gloom. Jacque went fishing for our supper. Jacque enjoyed fishing, so it was not work for him. CF would join him after he and Mike had a boxing lesson that Henry had promised them. Smith asked if he and I might continue our conversation from last night's supper since we were not doing any gold hunting the rest of the day.

"Nothing, I thought about what I said to you last night, and there are a few more things that I feel I should say," Smith began as we sat in the tent. "First of all, I have never slept so well in my life, since being in your group. The long workdays make me glad and ready for sleep. I also have never been so hungry in my life, and everything tastes so good when you are hungry. A song, a joke, a story, and Mike's ability to stir up both fun and tempers has kept life interesting. I wanted to admit to you honestly that my time with your group has been way better than being in jail," Smith said.

"Smith, you have won my respect for your willingness to work hard with us. We have all sensed that you want to leave us since we ran into the group of gold prospectors on the curve of the creek," I offered.

"It seems that I didn't keep my intentions covered very well. Did you see me talking to them about their partnership and asking if I could join them?" Smith asked me.

"No," I said. "It was CF, who sees everything, who saw you talking with the leaders of their group. CF told me, 'Smith like new men, he go with them. He no like us.'"

"I have good reasons for going with them," Smith said. "They travel with the expertise of two men who are knowledgeable about gold and mining. Until I get to Yale, I like the idea of being with a group where there would be better odds for success at finding gold. There is also no sharing of the treasure that is found. What you find, you keep. Every man for himself suits my style. It is a matter of me playing the better odds for success," Smith explained.

"For my part, I wish you well. This year, I search for gold so that I might have the resources to study medicine in London, England. So, I also search for gold for selfish reasons. My partnership with the others suits who I am. I value friends, deciding on our gold searching together, splitting equally whatever gold we find, and trusting those with me with my life," I explained.

Smith said frankly, "I've never trusted anyone else with my life, and I do not intend to risk my life for anyone but myself. I play in life without partners and always will. My question is—could there be a splitting of the gold we have found so I could get my equal share? I want to move on. When we go to the north end of the curve tomorrow, drop me off at their site. Could the group vote on my leaving at supper tonight?" Smith asked.

"I'll talk to Jacque about it right now," I said as I rose to leave to find Jacque at his fishing.

As a group, we were civil to Smith and his request to get his share of the gold collected and join the group we met on the creek. Some of us figured that Smith thought Frenchy and his brothers would keep following us and eventually get even with him. Mike was sure Smith had permission to run his Faro game with the other group. We had no resentment toward Smith. He had worked hard when he was with us and was welcome to move on as he desired. We left him with his new group on the creek the next morning.

The north end of the creek curve proved to have enough gold to keep us busy there for two days. By the end of the second day, we decided to vote about where we would next search for gold. As we passed Smith's group on the curve on our way home, they hailed us. They grimly said that Smith was wounded and dying, but there was no one there who cared about him. He had been shot the previous night over a Faro game. They said that we could take him and his stuff with us if we wanted. We were stunned! We had just left him with their group the day before yesterday.

We found Smith laying with a blood-soaked shirt on the ground with little alertness. He was shot in the back of his right hand and high in the front of his chest. Quickly, Mike and Henry picked him up and laid him in the canoe in my arms. Jacque and CF paddled as fast as possible to our camp, with Henry and Mike right behind us.

The only things going for Smith were that he was both young and fit. Who knew how much blood he had lost? The bullet in his chest needed to be removed. The other bullet had not gone through his right hand. It had plowed through the back in a nasty furrow, an ugly wound but not deadly. The gun shot to his chest was the matter of greater concern. By the time we had Smith laid out in the tent, he was unconscious.

I boiled water to sterilize my probe, scalpel, knife, and forceps. I told the others watching that I would irrigate or rinse the wound with a syringe of saltwater, and then I would probe the wound. If I could not detect the bullet without a great deal of effort, it might be better to leave it in his chest at least for a day or two.

Henry and Jacque held Smith steady so that he wouldn't move or thrash while I tried to locate the bullet in him. The bullet hadn't gone deep, and I was able to remove it. I sterilized the wound with rubbing alcohol and iodine after I sutured the wound closed. Then I put a dressing on it.

Smith had very shallow breathing but no sign of fever. I covered him well to make sure he was warm and watched over him. The others left the tent and tended the campfire. They worked together to prepare a supper of deer stew, so there would be broth for him if he woke up.

I would like to say Smith regained consciousness during the night, but he was dead by morning. Too many hours on the ground with no help. The anger in our group over Smith's senseless death was at a boiling point. We could not believe that no one had helped him, as a wounded man bleeding on the ground. At a somber breakfast, we discussed digging his grave and his funeral. Before we finished our meal, two men showed up from Smith's camp, asking if they could speak to us about what had happened to Smith. We invited them to say their piece.

They were scouts for the other group Smith had joined. Their names were Alf, short for Alfonzo, and Dino. Their Italian family roots were with the Northwest Fur Trading Company before merging with the Hudson's Bay Company. They were fur traders and woodsmen from Tacoma in the Washington area across the border. For the last two years, they traveled the Fraser River with gold rush groups that wanted guides. Increasingly, they were also asked to scout out creeks, rivers, and canyons connected to the Fraser as sources of gold. They had recognized Jacque as being connected to the Hudson's Bay Company. Jacque recognized them also, as trading at the Langley and Hope forts, where he had worked.

Establishing who they were made us more readily trust that they were telling us the truth. Alf began their story, "The day Smith arrived at camp, we had returned with a mountain goat carcass from back up the creek in the mountainous terrain. The two men who ran our group, Max Piketon and Rod Murdock, kept Smith to themselves and left with him to go to a different area away from our main group. They claimed that they had a lead on a reliable source of gold on the creek that they wanted to check out. The other miners asked me and Dino to follow Smith, the new guy, and our two bosses to see what they were doing.

They wanted us to follow them in the woods, and then spy on them with binoculars from the cover of the forest. That is what we did."

Before Alf and Dino could continue their story, we were interrupted by the arrival of Frenchy and his two brothers in one canoe and two other men in a second canoe. They guided their boats to shore while having loaded rifles pointed at us, demanding we hand over Smith.

Mike shouted for them to come ashore with their rifles lowered, and we would talk about handing Smith over to them. We told the two scouts to stay hidden in the tent while the rest of us filed out around Frenchy and his men, who were coming on shore.

Mike instructed Frenchy's group, "Keep your rifles lowered, we'll bring Smith's body to you, but he is dead. We were talking about digging his grave. You can help us dig it, and you can see with your own eyes that he is both truly dead and buried before you."

"Bring Smith to us, I don't believe what you say. Plus, dead or alive, we want him," Frenchy barked in his heavy French accent.

"We'll let you see that he's dead, but you are not taking him from here. Do you want to see that he is dead?" Mike snarled at Frenchy.

"We'll leave when we see that he is truly dead," Frenchy answered.

"Jacque and I will bring him out, so just stay where you are," Mike replied.

Myself, Henry, and CF eyed Frenchy and his men as we waited for Mike and Jacque to return with Smith. I whispered to them, "I don't trust Frenchy to do as he says."

Mike and Jacque returned, half dragging and carrying Smith's between them. Smith's head was hanging down. As they carried and dragged the body toward Frenchy and his men, I started screaming, "No, don't get Smith closer to Frenchy. You can't trust him!" As I was screaming, I grabbed Mike and tried to stop him from going further with Smith.

Mike tried to push me away with his one hand. I grabbed his arm and bent it into a hammer lock behind his back. "What is wrong with you, Nothing?" Mike bellowed in surprise and frustration.

CF had rushed up at the same time, grabbed Jacque, and yelled, "Frenchy, no good!" CF pulled Jacque's free arm, and his father lost his balance as he struggled to keep a hold of Smith.

Both CF and I struggled with Mike and Jacque, and they let go of their grip on Smith's body, which began to fall. Frenchy's two brothers rushed up and grabbed Smith before his body reached the ground. They rushed to their canoe with Smith and threw him in it, then jumped in themselves. With one at either end of it, they proceeded to row away.

Frenchy and the others with him also ran for their other canoe. Henry yelled at the four of us struggling with each other, "Stop fighting! They're getting away with Smith!" Henry ran to the river and screamed, "Stop!" His shout only made the departing go faster. He fired five times at them from onshore, and three times when we chased them by our boats.

We didn't pursue them far in our canoes. They had taken Smith, who they had wanted alive, not as a dead man. When we returned to shore, the two scouts were waiting for us, looking puzzled.

Mike and Jacque were less than happy toward me and CF after our interference. We were not happy with them either, and the four of us were not ready to do anything but yap at each other in red hot frustration.

"Better stay in the tent," Henry said to the two scouts. "The four of them have to clear the air between them. I'll wait there with you while I keep an eye on them."

Clearing the air is best described by very vague terms. Typically, it involved heated verbal accusations, name calling, and colorful judgments. In this the case, Mike was vexed at me, and I at him. It resulted in insults while he was chasing me, and I was dodging him. In this particular clearing the air incident, there was Indian wrestling between CF and Jacque.

Clearing the air might end with at least one person being thrown in the river. After a shorter or longer duration of time, those involved in clearing the air would shake hands and go about life, as if there was never a disagreement or cross word said between them. We found that we could not be together in good humor without a chance to express our frustration and differences of opinions with each other now and again. Usually, one or more persons in our group did not take part in a session on clearing the air. It was their job to call it off if it became more harmful than helpful. We called it horseplay or blowing off steam. Henry referred to it as us simply acting like asses.

On this particular day, our clearing of the air was brief. We four got to the tent, and Henry shook his head at us. The two scouts had genuine smiles for our antics. Jacque said to the scouts, "Go ahead and finish your story of what happened to Smith at your camp."

They continued, "We followed the three of them, our bosses and Smith, as they travelled along the creek past the middle of the curve. We wondered if he would lead them to your group, but they stopped soon after the middle, at the sand and fine gravel area. Smith made a large circle including the creek shore and the sand and gravel running beside it. Then our bosses went to work, searching for gold along with Smith. Down from the tree line was a deep hollow nearer the place the three were searching for gold. Dino crawled into it to hear what they were saying."

Henry interrupted their story, blurting out, "I bet Smith was telling them that it was where we found gold nuggets."

Dino responded, "Yes, they were talking about finding gold in that area." He continued, "As the day went on, and they did not have any success, the bosses accused Smith of lying to them. He swore to them that he wasn't. He reminded them that he hadn't promised them they would find a jackpot. He had only promised to show them where his group had found nuggets. Max, the meanest of the two bosses, pulled a pistol and demanded Smith show them some gold nuggets to prove his story.

"Are your bosses always this demanding and suspicious?" I asked the two men.

"They are if it involves anything to do with gold or money," Alf answered.

Dino said, "They knew that they had met their match in Smith because they could see that he wasn't afraid of them and wouldn't give up his gold without a fight. Smith told them that he had to get his gold bag from his underwear to show them his nuggets. He was calm and showed no fear.

"He prided himself in getting the better of others," I spoke out.

"He almost did best them," Dino replied. He then continued explaining, "Smith had turned around from facing them with his hands up high, and then slowly lowered them while saying that he was just undoing his pants and grabbing his gold bag from his underwear. He raised his gold bag up, high in his left hand, then said, "See, here it is for you to check." At the same time, he turned around quickly with a small derringer, and he shot just a second faster than Max. His shot caught Max between the eyes. Max's shot sent a bullet across Smith's right hand. Smith dropped his gun but picked it up with his left hand and fired at the second boss named Rod. He missed him. Rod had his gun out and ready and shot Smith in the upper chest in the collar bone area. Smith went down and did not come up."

"Did you know Max and Rod were such cold-blood devils before this?" Henry asked the men.

"I guess we knew they might be, but before Smith, we hadn't seen them in action before our eyes," Alf said. "It was shocking," he continued, "To see Rod act as such a swine. After shooting Smith, he picked up Smith's gun, and then his gold pouch. He looked at the two gold nuggets in it. After he admired them, he put them back in the pouch, and then it went into his pocket. He searched Smith's pockets for any other valuables and did the same to Max. After searching the dying and dead, Rod started back toward our camp, and we hurried through the woods to get back before him."

"You mean this Rod just left Smith lying there on the ground with a bullet in him? He didn't care if he was alive or dead?" Mean Mike asked in disbelief.

Dino answered, "No, he didn't care. When he got to camp, he announced Max had left on a business venture and would not be back anytime soon. Rod also announced that Smith was wounded in an accident and that the scouts, meaning us, would go out and bring him back to camp. He told us to follow the creek in our canoe until we saw Smith on the shore and bring him back to camp, but we were not to go until after supper. Rod also sent bow-legged Bill and Old Kelly in another canoe on a job that involved them carrying a shovel and spade with them. At sunset, Rod sent us to pick up Smith and return him to camp. When we got back with Smith, Rod had us put him in Max's tent. We tried to come back to Max's tent with water and bandages for Smith's hand and chest, but bow-legged Bill was guarding the tent and told us to stay away from it on Rod's orders."

Alf continued, "In the morning, we had the mountain goat carcass to cut up with half of it to hang over a smoking fire. Rod told us to help pan for gold when the goat meat was taken care of, and firewood collected for the evening. We asked Rod if Smith was okay. He said that he was dying, but there was no one there to care for him. We suggested that we go to your camp and see if you would tend to him, but Rod refused. He said that if Smith was still alive when you went by in the evening, we could ask you then. Smith was barely alive when you picked him up yesterday. We could not help him much, but we wanted you to know how it all played out for him. We also want to warn you that Rod, having stolen Smith's gold nuggets, will be planning on getting yours. We advise you to stay clear of him and post a guard at night."

Before the two scouts could leave our camp, a canoe came near with a white peace flag flying. It was Frenchy's two brothers, who came about ten feet from shore and tossed Smith's body in the water, and then took off without any words. Mike waded out in the river and retrieved the body.

Alf and Dino said, "We will help you dig a grave." They not only helped dig Smith's grave, but they stayed for his burial. We wrapped in a blanket, and then lowered his body into the ground.

Once in his grave, I read from Psalm 130: "Out of the depths I cry to you O Lord, hear my voice. Let your ears be attentive to my cry for mercy. We come to you with broken spirits and contrite hearts as we bury this man we know only as Smith. We praise your name Lord in life and death. In Smith's last hours, he suffered, forsaken and alone. Your Son Jesus Christ suffered for us sinners forsaken on his cross, may Christ's suffering grant Smith mercy before you. Have mercy on us all. Amen."

We then said The Lord's Prayer together, and when it ended, Henry began to sing the song that we had all sung together first at the mudflats and several times afterward. Every one of us joined in singing even Alf and Dino.

We then took turns filling in Smith's grave in silence, and there wasn't a dry eye among us. Smith didn't want friends, but we shed tears for his violent and forsaken end. My hope was that Smith might have at last partnered up with God when he found himself wounded, helpless, and completely alone in his last hours.

CHAPTER EIGHT:

The Odds of Finding More Than Crumbs of Gold

IT WAS LATE afternoon when Smith's burial was finished, and we invited Alf and Dino to eat with us before they headed back to their camp. Our guests suggested that our early evening was favorable for fishing. If we had fish for our supper, they wanted to show us how to fillet so that every bone was gone. Being on the boastful side, the brothers also wanted to demonstrate how to make a flour paste-like-sauce to dip the fillets in before frying them to perfection in a large amount of bubbling hot bacon grease. We were happy if they wanted to show us how good they were at preparing and cooking fresh fish. At first, the fish were not cooperative with our supper plans, but we did end up catching more than enough for supper.

Alf and Dino exceeded their boasting. Their battered and fried boneless fillets were a mouth-watering treat. Not to be outdone, CF produced extra tasty bannocks and a scrumptious rice pudding flavored with dried apples and honey. It was a special meal of laughter and new friendship. As we sat about the campfire, Henry played his flute and directed us into a choir, with CF keeping our tempo upbeat with a clear drumbeat.

Henry was an expert at encouraging our singing, as if we each had notable talent. He identified Alf and Dino as altos, Mike and Henry as tenors, me and CF as baritones, and Jacque as our fine bass. Sometimes an evening turns into unexpected delight, which seasons your memory for days to come, and this was one of those.

The next morning, we decided to pause and take a look at our plans for continuing our gold searching up the Fraser. As we went about breaking camp, we discussed Smith's opinion that we were too relaxed and not greedy enough. We decided to seriously consider our chances of success and respond to Smith's biggest grievance.

The Faro dealer's greatest irritation was that Jacque kept all the gold to be split equally. We had each agreed that Jacque should hold our gold as we retrieved it, as he was the best among us at recognizing what was real and what was look a-like. Jacque was as good as having an assayer in our group. If he had a doubt about anything collected, he kept it separate and had an actual assayer check out its value. Yet, he was seldom wrong about what was authentic. Sharing whatever gold was found among us equally prevented jealousy and resentments, to which none of us were immune.

Gold dust—particles of grains, flakes, and pellets—were small, but they added up over each day, week, and month into value for each of us. Small to tiny gold nuggets were common. They sometimes came in bunches, but the impressive sized nuggets that Smith went nuts over tended to materialize only now and again. Nuggets combined with gold dust were the difference between success and failure. The best success was to be the first to find a deposit of gold and get all the gold for yourself or group. That was why people filed mining claims.

None of us wanted to be part of hard rock mining, working in mines underground extracting gold ore so it could be refined into gold ingots. No one in our group had money to invest in lode mining, and we were content to be searching for placer gold. The Fraser River was infested with gold prospectors like us because it had shoals or sand and gravel bars, rich in gold deposits. Placer gold was available to those who were willing to sift through the sand, gravel, and mud to separate the pieces of gold from its natural neighbors. Some bars in the Fraser were richer in gold deposits than others. Hill's Bar, near Yale, was a rich gravel bar of placer gold where many found significant wealth, but by the previous year it had been covered by mining claims.

Miners were determined to follow the Fraser until they could find the origin of the gold from which the particles and nuggets had eroded and then been transported by the river's currents to the various sand bars, obstructions, bends, and depressions in the Fraser's riverbed. The race was on to travel the Fraser River to get to its various gold deposits before others, and that meant going farther and farther upriver and even inland following rivers or creeks emptying into the Fraser.

The gold rush had begun in 1858; now it was 1860, and we were traveling over already mined portions of the mighty river. Deposits of placer gold were not usually so deep and intense that they could not be exhausted after months or a year of sifting through them. Then again, a good amount of gold could sometimes be found after others had already looked for it on a gravel bar. The Fraser River had a fickle nature, ever uncovering and covering its sand and gravel bars and playing 'now you see gold, now you don't.'

On our first trip, we had not traveled farther than Yale on the Fraser River, but this time we were aiming for beyond Yale to places already famous for gold deposits, and then farther up the Fraser as far as fate would allow. According to Alf and Dino, mining claims on Hill's Bar and Boston Bar might now be purchased, as the push for gold was farther and farther up the Fraser and on to creeks and rivers flowing into it. The gamble in buying a claim was that the odds of finding more gold could be small. Would a miner leave a good paying claim? The price of the claim was a key factor.

This year, even with an early start, three of us knew from experience that the weather, the ever-changing water level, the force of the current in the Fraser, and the competition from the number of other gold searchers were all variables to our success. Old Man Magee had helped us learn the value of a rocker. This time, we would need to consider the use of a sluice box as well. We needed to keep learning from the example of others along the river as to how we could best get the gold that was there.

When we had our camp taken down and were ready to leave, CF suggested we have a meeting, as he was accustomed to seeing the chief of his tribe and his council holding. He also said the chief trader at the Hudson's Bay Company fort often called some of his employees together for a talk. In his tribe, it was a face-to-face meeting with the chief in a circle, sometimes with a ritual passing of the pipe, but often simply just a talk about concerns of the current life and wellbeing of the tribe. The chief invited people to speak to him about what he wanted them to discuss. The chief at the fort and the chief of the tribe listened to others, and then they followed what they thought was the best course of action.

When CF suggested a sit-down meeting, the rest of us were once again impressed with his wisdom and maturity. I agreed, "Yes, let's have a meeting. The killing of Smith reminds us that our safety and success is in our partnership. Two people together are stronger than one person alone. The five of us together are two doubled plus one more which means we are powerful."

"I agree that a few minutes of talking together is a promising idea. I suggest that CF act as our chief or chief trader," Henry offered, echoing my approval of a meeting.

"Let's get her done!" Mean Mike said approvingly as he sat down on the ground, adding, "Sit down in a circle, lads. CF, get this conflab started."

As he sat down with the rest of us, CF said, "What conflab mean?"

"It means talking together, and CF in the twenty-two days we have been together, you have been quick in learning to talk more fully with us. You have a gift for languages, as you also have a good understanding of a number of French words," Henry said sincerely.

CF said with a sly grin, "Now I mighty chief." In a more serious tone, he continued, "Why you want gold? Mike, you talk."

Without hesitation, Mike stated, "I want to be rich."

CF said to Mike, "Still talk."

"Everybody wants to be rich. Gold can buy ye anythin'. It gives ye power and respect. With enough money, ye never have to work," Mike responded.

CF asked Mike rapid-fire. "You hate work? You no power no respect without gold?"

"No, I don't hate work. Yes, I have power and respect without gold. But CF, or Chief, in the White man's world the more gold ye have the better off ye are," Mike answered.

CF said to Mike, "Last year, you, Nothing, and Jacque got gold. Nothing and Jacque say their gold from last year nest egg. Gold for doctor school for Nothing. Jacque want ranch. What you do gold?"

"My gold was for a business, a blacksmith shop or general store, but I drank and gambled it away. I liked spending it while it lasted. Now, I want to get gold again, as I'm at broke," Mike stated, frankly.

Next, CF spoke to Henry. "Why you want gold?"

"I am not so different from Mike. I'm also just barely above broke. In England, where I hail from, I am a third son of an old family. Our family estate, or barony, is crumbling because of lack of wealth. There is nothing of substance behind the title." Henry went on to explain, "There is an order of British nobility. King or Queen at the top, then in the order of Duke, Marquess, Earl, Viscount, and last, but not least, Baron. However, peerage and ranking in the nobility is no guarantee of wealth. Moreover, titles and heredity can be suffocating and shackled to rules and etiquette that crushes one's very soul. Here in this frontier, I have the freedom of being a commoner, making my own future by daring and arduous work. Here is wilderness and land as God designed it. Here after twenty-two days, I have some gold. The start of my nest egg."

CF spoke to Jacque. "Gold collected enough. Yes? No?"

Jacque held up his hands and shrugged, saying, "There is no answer. We are off to a good start, but each of you must decide if it is enough or not. Smith felt it was too little for our effort. We did well last year over time. No one knows what this year will become; enough gold or too little."

CF asked, "Need more meat? Need other stuff? All talk now."

"If someone is going hunting for game, I would like to go along. In

England, we used dogs to hunt. I should like to see hunting here without dogs," Henry spoke up, and then added, "The deer meat is almost used up. Someone needs to hunt."

CF asked, "Hunt now? New camp?"

"New camp," Mike said, then added, "If you, Chief, agree?"

"Here need all agree," CF stated bluntly. "Put hand up, hunt new camp?" All hands went up.

CF asked, "All want get gold? Put hand up." All hands went up again. CF said, "Talk done."

"Well done, Chief," we all congratulated CF.

CF said, "I no real chief. Chief, big boss. No hand up before him."

With those words, we set off up the Fraser River in search of gravel bars on our pursuit for gold. We traveled most of the day without success until late afternoon, when we spotted a small empty gravel bar close to a spot on the riverbank that was suitable for our camp. Jacque and CF set up while Mike, Henry, and I began panning on the gravel bar. Mike, preferring the rocker, worked it himself while Henry and I worked with our gold pans. Mike had good success with the rocker, and both Henry and I were collecting small particles of gold. We were excited when Jacque came in a canoe to call us back to camp for supper. Since we seemed to be at a good spot, Jacque said he would stay there and work while we had supper, and then we could come back so he could get his evening meal.

We ate quickly, eager to get back to the bar. Jacque had good luck finding gold while we were gone. We lit a campfire on the bar when it got dark, and Mike and Jacque said they were willing to spend the night there. It was too rich in gold to leave for someone else to claim. The dawn found us sharing tea and porridge on the gravel bar, anxious to find as much gold as soon as possible. Our spirits were high and about midmorning, a canoe with one lone person in it headed for our sandbar.

As the canoe drew closer, we saw that a big man was paddling it with his partner, a bluetick coonhound. The man had a big smile as bright as the sun. "Gentlemen," he called, "The name is Limon Jim. Could I come ashore and stretch my legs?" Before we could respond, he continued, "My dog would also like to run. His name's King. He will need about two minutes of loud barking time when we exit the canoe to make sure you are aware of his presence. He will show off how fast he can run as he yelps like thunder, but he will not bite or attack any of you even if you are a damn Yankee way up here in this British hell hole."

Mike yelled, "Come ashore both of ye!" We watched as a giant of a man, slightly taller and even broader than Mean Mike, came toward us from his beached canoe.

He greeted us in a loud booming voice with a slight hint of a French accent, "My name is James Limon. Limon, my last name, is a French word meaning the citrus fruit. Being the part owner of a sugar plantation and sugar being the opposite of sour lemons, I have

81

been branded most of my life with the title, Lemon Jim. King and I appreciate being able to take a break in our travels. Okay King, have a run."

King jumped out the canoe when his owner instructed him. Until then, King had stayed quietly beside his master without any sound. Upon Lemon Jim's command to have a run, the bluetick coonhound raced all around the gravel bar. King had a distinctive hound sounding bark as he raced back and forth on our small sandbar. We all watched the dog and his delight as he stretched his legs in boundless joy.

Lemon Jim informed us that bluetick coonhounds are a fixture of his parish in Louisiana. His pride of ownership of King was evident when he announced, "There ain't no finer hunting dog in the world. A bluetick coonhound can pursue and tree about any creature it finds. It has been known to chase cougars and mountain lions. It is a cold nose tracker. That is, dogs like King can sniff out trails that have gone cold for hours, and even days."

All of us were impressed with the dog, but Mean Mike, who loved dogs of every kind, asked Lemon Jim, "Is King full growd or will he grow bigger?"

Lemon Jim reported that King was twenty-seven inches in height, as high as the breed gets, and that he weighed at a give-or-take seventy pounds.

Mean Mike said in admiration of King, "Look laddies, at such a short, sleek, dark blue coat with molted black spots on the back and ears. He even has a tan spot or two. I've never seen the likes of him. I would love to see him hunt."

"So would I," Henry chimed in enthusiastically.

"I would consider it an honor to show you gentlemen King's skill and intelligence in hunting if you have the time," Lemon Jim offered.

Henry spoke up, "We have to vote on it." Then he loudly asked, "Can Mike and I go off and see this dog hunt for a couple of hours? Hands up if you are okay with it." The other three of us gave our approval. Henry said to a surprised Lemon Jim, "Let's go, but we need to stop at our camp first. Follow our canoe." Mike and Henry jumped in one of our canoes and were off, and Lemon Jim and King were hard-pressed to keep up to their hasty departure.

I said to Jacque and CF, "Mike and Henry fell for the temptation and were easily lured away by a fine-looking hunting dog. I thought it would have been a pretty lady. I hope they don't get their hearts broken."

"With Mike along in a hunting party you may as well have a barking dog," Jacque said.

"I hope my crow is safe," CF offered.

We worked through our lunch break, expecting the hunting party back at any time, waiting to eat and rest with them. When that never happened, we ate, noting the couple of hours kept growing. We were well into the late afternoon when the three hunters and King returned. Lemon Jim was no longer smiling like the sun, and Henry and Mean Mike looked like they had bitten off the head of a rattlesnake. Riding majestically in a canoe paddled by his servant, Lemon Jim, the bluetick coonhound looked as handsome as ever.

As the two boats drew near, we had the feeling the hunting expedition had turned sour. Lemon Jim got out of his canoe and stood beside it. Mike and Henry had jumped from their canoe and stood beside him. I called to them as they gathered by Lemon Jim, "I hope you got a good amount of meat."

"Not exactly," Lemon Jim said. He continued in his loud voice but with a perturbed edge to it. "I just wanted to go on my way but after a physical intimidation by these two culprits, I am forced to confess that I killed a crow in a demonstration of my pistol shooting skills. It seems it's a pet of one of you, and I am responsible for its death. Now that I have confessed to the murder of this crow before its owner and you all, I will leave your presence with great distaste." To Mike and Henry, he said, "You two thugs have my eternal loathing and animosity." Lemon Jim left in his canoe, never looking back at us. As he went, we were all staring at CF, waiting for a response to Lemon Jim's confession.

It was the longest silence all of us ever endured. CF's face was as stone, and his body was straight and tall like a plank board. Mike lumbered ashore and marched up to CF. "I'm truly sorry, lad. We didn't know what he intended to shoot when he said he would show us that he was as good with his pistol as with his rifle. He said, 'Watch me shoot the small knot on that tree trunk over there,' and he hit the knot with his pistol shot. Then he said, 'See the pinecone second branch from the treetop,' and he hit it with his pistol shot. A crow flew from a lower branch on his second shot, and Lemon Jim said, 'I can shoot a bird in flight.' We screamed, 'Don't shoot,' but he ignored us. He fired two times to make sure he got the crow, hitting it both times. We knew by how the bird flew that it was yours. We got the body and put it in a safe spot, so you can see your bird at camp." Henry had joined Mean Mike, standing beside him as he told CF what had happened. We could see both men were genuinely stricken that the events had turned deadly for CF's crow.

Finally, CF spoke when Mean Mike ended his account of the crow's death. "The men of my people no cry at death. The women cry, wail, make noise, honor dead one. Crow no person. Good bird friend in life. Now spirit friend in death. His feather I will carry with me always. Death come any day, not stop it. Not you fault."

A huge sigh went through us all at CF's answer. This brave young man was so wise and mature about life and death. In the same way, we had been impressed with his maturity and honesty after our sit-down meeting when we had asked him why he wanted gold.

He had looked at us and said, "I no want gold. I take it. Use it to trade maybe. I no like mud digging. I like you, White men. Make me smile on face and inside." We were sure pleased CF was with us.

We suggested that Jacque and CF prepare our evening meal and bring it to the gravel bar, as well as wood for the campfire. Henry and I volunteered to sleep on the bar overnight. We wanted CF to have more private time with his dead crow and the taking of a feather for himself. Everyone wanted to hear about the hunting with King and Lemon Jim, but we agreed the story would be dessert for supper. Mean Mike and Henry threw themselves into gold searching and remained unusually closed mouthed about their hunting experience.

When Jacque and CF arrived at the gravel bar with rabbit stew, we knew their hunting trip had been successful on some level. Hungry men talk little and eat fast, and that was our supper. So, in no time flat, we devoured every speck of stew with every biscuit crumb. Mike and Henry were reluctant to tell every detail of their encounter with Lemon Jim and King, but it was with lynching pressure from the other three of us that Henry began the first part of their story.

Henry said, "Both Mike and I wanted to see King in action and expected that Lemon Jim would treat such a beautiful dog with a masterful hand. At camp, we picked up our rifles and joined the man and the bluetick coonhound, ready to see the dog hunt. Lemon Jim was intent on showing us his rifle and its precision for long distance accuracy. In Lemon's long-winded bragging about his gun, he had leashed King to a tree branch with the command to sit and not move. It became evident that Lemon Jim expected not only the dog but Mike and I to listen and not move until he finished demonstrating his extraordinary rifle and what he called his close-shot hunting pistol. In Lemon's last rifle shot, he was so busy sighting the weapon that he almost stepped on top of King, who moved out of the way, startling Lemon Jim, and his shot was not on target as he wanted."

Mean Mike cut in, a voice full of anger, "And Lemon screamed at King to, 'Sit!' I thought he started to raise his fist and that he was going to hit the dog for having moved without being told to. I yelled at Lemon, 'Do ye know the dog had to move or ye would of stepped on him?' And the nitwit said, 'Obedience always comes first, for dog or man in spite of any circumstance. Let me show you that I'm as good a shot with my pistol as with my rifle.' Henry take over telling the story while I cool my temper."

I spoke up before Henry could continue. "Do you think Lemon hits his dog for the smallest reason, when he is angry?"

Mean Mike muttered, "I wouldn't put it past him."

Henry began, "You already know it got worse with Lemon demonstrating his skill with his pistol, resulting in the killing of CF's crow. What we didn't tell you was how we reacted when Lemon ignored us and shot the bird. When the crow fell to the ground, we both raced to it, wishing there was hope for it, but both shots had robbed it of any thread of life. Seeing our concern over the dead crow,

Lemon asked, 'Is there a problem with the bird?'"

Mean Mike clamored, "Let me tell you how I answered him. I roared, 'Yes, there is a problem! Are ye deaf or just stupid? We told ye not to shoot at the crow!' Then that halfwit Lemon said, 'I heard you, but I thought you must have been joking. How could a crow be of any value to anyone?' Henry jumped in front of me, so I could not go charging toward Lemon, and said, 'This crow was a pet of one of our men. It will be a sad and needless loss to him.' Lemon was completely indifferent. All he said was, 'There are endless crows around. He can make a pet of another.' 'With hostility, I asked Lemon, 'He should make another pet? Why? So, you can murder it too?' Lemon Jim enjoyed my anger and outrage. Wouldn't you agree?" Mean Mike asked Henry.

Henry answered Mean Mike, "Lemon Jim purposely tried to aggravate us as the owner of a fine hunting dog." Henry then continued to say, "Lemon presented his guns and his dog to us, to glorify himself. At first, I tried to give Lemon the benefit of the doubt that he just had immense pride in his dog and guns, but the more we were with him, the more I saw he was just full of himself. He was too wrapped up in himself to see the intelligence and talents of his dog or the advantage that fine weapons give to the person firing them."

Jacque questioned, "Do you think Lemon may have a slave owner mentality that he is entitled to own people, animals, and things and that they show how superior he is in his own mind?"

Mean Mike answered, "Well, Lemon Jim does seem to think he is above others and if they don't see how great he is, he rejects them as too dimwitted to matter."

Henry said, "Let me get this story told. Lemon led us into the woods, removed King's leash, and said to him, 'Go hunt.' The dog walked all about the area we were in, sniffing the ground. After a couple of minutes, the dog then took off on a trot still sniffing. Soon, King was out of sight. I asked Lemon Jim, 'Aren't we following the dog?' and Lemon answered, 'He will be back soon enough. If he needs help, he will bark.'"

Mike spoke up, "King was impressive! When sent on his own to hunt, he returned with a fine rabbit. After dropping it at Lemon's feet, he bounded off again. King returned in a brief time with a second dead rabbit that he again brought to Lemon Jim. Lemon announced that the dog would next tree a bigger animal for our hunting success, but he needed to return to his canoe for his snuff box. So, we said that there was no problem waiting for him. We were glad Lemon was gone for a bit, as it gave us time to pet and praise King. We were amazed at how the dog laid still, waiting for his master. The dog seemed afraid to move since he had been given the command to lie down while his owner was gone. We both had deer jerky and fed King bits of it. Henry poured a little water from his canteen in the cup of his hand, and King licked it."

Henry took over telling their story, saying, "We had some fine moments with the dog until Lemon Jim returned, wearing a shiny smile that seemed phoney because he turned it off and on like flies that come and go on dead meat. Showing his dog, no affection or kind words, Lemon just announced, 'Get up, King, we are hunting game.'

This time, he put the coonhound on the leash and walked behind him until King began to pull in a particular direction. We followed the two about a hundred feet, and then Lemon Jim let King off his leash again. King trotted off, the three of us trailing behind. When he disappeared from view, we followed in the general direction he had gone. Then Lemon said to us, 'We wait to hear from King. Do not move or speak.'"

Jacque interrupted Henry, 'What did Mike do in the silence? I bet he whistled to himself, loudly belched now and again, and farted at least twice, loud enough to shame a horse."

Mean Mike spoke out, "Ye know the only time I be silent is when I'm passed out drunk."

Mike's words were met with scoffing and objections such as, "You snore in your sleep when drunk!" "You talk and yell in your sleep whether you're drunk or sober!" and "You fart like a horse even then!"

Laughing, Henry said, "Back to the hunting story. After waiting in silence for what felt a painfully long time, we could hear King barking, and Lemon was good at sensing the direction the sound was coming from. Before long, we came upon King barking at a racoon in a tree."

After a drink of water, Henry continued, "Lemon asked us, 'Do you eat racoon or collect its pelt?' Being new to the wilderness, I didn't know, but Mike said, 'Usually only if game is really scarce.'

Boy, Lemon didn't like to hear that and became very impatient with us, and he asked, 'Do you want to shoot it or not?' Then snarling, he added, 'Did you come to hunt or to fart?' You can be sure Mike reacted to Lemon's sour tone toward us by saying, 'This time, we'll just fart.'"

CF spoke up excitedly, "Lemon Jim bossy, snappy, man like chief trader at fort."

Henry agreed that Lemon Jim was both bossy and snappy. Henry continued, "When Mike said that this time, we'll just fart, Lemon snapped with anger in his voice, like he could shoot anything that moved, 'Fine with me!' Then he yelled, 'Heel, King!' and the dog stopped barking at the raccoon instantly and went and sat without a sound beside his master.

So, Mike then said to Lemon, 'Sorry to anger you, but raccoon meat can need careful preparing. It may need boiling in water, and then roasting. It also tends to be fatty. Hunger will demand ye eat what's there, but not every animal's a first choice for meat.'

Henry was caught up in telling the story, but he was running out of voice as he continued, "Lemon Jim acted like he was ignoring Mike's explanation, but then he said in belligerence to King, 'These men hunt only meat that is a delicacy. We will continue hunting.' As we left, Lemon Jim put King on his leash and lead him and us off in another direction. After a time of walking, King indicated that his sniffing of the ground had him eager to go after another animal. Mike, you can take a turn at telling what happened next."

"Lemon Jim let the dog off his leash and before long, Lemon was leading us to another animal that King had cornered or treed. When we caught up to the coonhound, we saw it was a fine beaver. Lemon Jim said, 'Gentlemen, here is a beaver, a source of meat, and a tail that is a delicacy. Since you may still be reluctant to shoot, I will have King attack the beaver if you do not object.' I said to Lemon Jim, 'I'm sure King will kill the beaver, but the beaver has four powerful front teeth, and in a fight, the beaver may wound King badly, so let us shoot it.' But Lemon only got defensive at my advice. He snapped at me in irritation, 'You forget yourself, sir. King is my dog to do as I bid him. If I want him to fight the beaver, then it is no concern of yours!'"

"A person like Lemon shouldn't be allowed to own any dog," I said, and Henry, Jacque, and CF all chorused. "Damn right."

Mean Mike shook his head in agreement and continued telling the story. "Henry tried to get Lemon to consider the safety of his dog. He said, 'Sir, we understand King is your dog, but would you needlessly endanger him without compelling cause?' And at that, Lemon exploded, yelling, 'Fine!' as he pulled out his pistol and shot the beaver. He had two bullets left in the gun and also put them into the animal.

Looking at us, Lemon said icily, 'You, gentlemen, tire my patience. Let us return to your camp.'

As we began to return to camp, I said to Lemon, 'We have seen ye have a great hunting dog both well trained and intelligent. Ye be fortunate to have such a valuable animal.' Henry also added, 'I agree. I could see CF and Jacque in our group using such a dog in hunting with enormous success.'

Mike continued, "Lemon Jim then said, 'I presume you mean the older and younger two breeds in your group hunting with a dog like King. It is my experience that like slaves, breeds cannot be trusted. As a slave buyer, I must judge the value of slaves on their appearance. I can see an independent and rebellious spirit in the eyes of those two with you.'"

Jacque spoke up, "I am independent in spirit, and I would be rebellious if I was a slave of his."

CF added, "I fox spirit, too smart for White Lemon Jim!"

Mike said, "I told Lemon, 'Jacque and CF are trusted partners. I trust them with my life. We're both partners and friends. We don't call them breeds. We call them brothers. The fact that they are both of White and Native blood is not a sin or disgrace. They are trustworthy because we trust them, and they trust us.' Lemon looked at me like I was saying nothing worth hearing.

I decided it was time for me to ask Lemon Jim if he would part with his dog, so I asked, 'Would ye consider selling yer dog?'

'Only for a gold ransom,' Lemon answered me. I had to agree with him and said, 'Well, from what I've seen, King is worth one.'

CF spoke out, "Good thing, Mike, to have great hunting dog!"

When we reached our camp, I wasn't ready when Lemon Jim said that he might consider a more reasonable price if I beat him in arm wrestling. Lemon bragged that he had broken an opponent's arm in a match before, so I should be forewarned.

"Sounds like Lemon has a pure mean streak and would break a fellow's arm just to prove how strong he is," Jacque said.

Mean Mike replied, "That is what I thought too, but I replied to Lemon, 'You be forewarned, as I have bent a cold horseshoe in my bare hands to fit a horse's foot. Let's get to the arm wrestling unless you're afraid.'"

Henry took over the story, saying, "The two of them decided they needed to build a platform upon which they could compete. First, they picked out a sturdy young tree and cut the top off at a suitable height for them to rest their arms. The only straight board in camp was my ironing board, which they nailed to the top of the cut-off tree. When Mike and Lemon's elbows were in position and their big meaty hands clasped, I said, 'Begin.' Both men were determined to win, and the sounds of grunting and straining filled the air. When Mike brought Lemon's arm down in victory, Lemon was mortified.

He had not lost at arm wrestling in so long—or maybe ever—that he was stricken with defeat.

Henry paused speaking, shook his head, and said, "I was actually a bit sorry for Lemon, his loss of pride in himself was painful to see."

I said, "We have all been knocked off our high opinion of our ability, and it takes time to gather up the pieces. It is never fun to feel defeated."

Henry nodded his head and said that Mike was more than decent, saying to Lemon, "Ye be one of the best at arm wrestling. I respect the owner of any dog, there is no pressure from me to buy him.' I could see Mike's words turned Lemon red in anger, but he managed to spit out a curt, 'Thank you.' I don't feel that I am really a great marksman, but I asked Lemon if maybe a pistol shooting competition would help his mood?"

Mike spoke up, "When Lemon asked Henry what he had in mind, I could see that Lemon was ready to jump at his offer to prove his superiority over us another way."

Henry said, I explained to Lemon, "We get three pistol shots each at your snuff box, as a target inside my gold pouch. We tie the bag to a tree limb and from thirty feet away, we shoot to break the string holding the pouch. Whoever brings it down by hitting the string wins the competition! If you win, you get my gold pouch, which has a little gold in it. If I win, you can have your snuff box back, but you must apologize to the owner of the pet crow at the sand bar."

Henry said to Mike, "You tell them about the shooting challenge. Mike reported, "The shooting competition took a while. After the first time both Henry and Lemon had fired their three shots, the pouch was hanging securely to the tree. After the second time each had their three shots, the pouch was still suspended tightly. Lemon was getting frustrated, and he snapped, 'This could take all damn day.' To that, Henry said, 'That's fine by me,' which I could see only added to Lemon's impatience. The pistol contest continued and on

Henry's second shot, he hit the string and brought the pouch down from the tree limb. He went and picked up the pouch, took Lemon's snuff box out it, and handed it to Lemon. Lemon Jim said, 'Let's go to your sand bar, I cannot stand your company any longer,' and you were here to receive Lemon Jim's apology."

CF spoke first, "Mike, dog should be yours! You won arm-wrestle."

"I think someone like Lemon Jim will cross our path again. He is like unwelcome news that catches up with you," I stated.

Jacque said, "We meet people from all over the world in this gold rush. They bring hate and greed with them. When the gold is gone, I hope they will go home."

Henry exclaimed, "I hope we don't become hateful and greedy ourselves. I suggest if one of us is getting that way, we have Mean Mike sit on him and squeeze the hate and greed out of him."

Mean Mike said, "Too bad we didn't do that to Smith."

CHAPTER NINE:

Closing in on Yale

AT LEAST LEMON Jim and King's visit made a diversion of topic for conversation as we continued our search for gold on the gravel bar. We were pleased with the steady, modest amount we found. To Smith, it would not have been enough for all our work invested, but to us, we were willing to work hard to share a little gold day by day. The river did not owe us or anyone gold, and we respected that the Fraser offered it to those who dared to look for it and worked hard to take it.

Old Man Magee had loved the Fraser because of its mysterious, rough, and primitive nature. He recognized a long and strong-willed river of danger and death. Magee often fished there for its gift of bountiful salmon, and he was one with the native fishermen of eons. Yet, much as he admired and respected the mighty Fraser, he wrote a poem about its devilish side. I would often quote all or part of it to the others. Mean Mike insisted I had mixed up something in the poem, but he could not say what I had changed. In spite of this, I would routinely recite the words to fill the long silences when canoeing or panning for gold, while the river lapped about us and mocked our presence there.

Henry asked me to recite the poem as we headed for our camp that night. It was later evening, and much of the daylight had slipped away on us as I offered my recitation of Old Man Magee's poem.

The Fraser
Dirty brown river hurrying along,
Filled with mean pride and spirit.
Treacherous water, tempting with hidden gold.

Homegrown, back in mountain peaks,
A razor cutting rock and pushing land,
Bending and stretching in long winding flow,
To empty in the ocean far distance below.

Scorning us foolish folk–Here

To poke and choke out your gold.
You have laid the get rich snare,
Ready to watch us die trying.

No sooner than I ended my recitation, our canoe hit something in the water. CF, Henry, and me were in the boat, near the shore of our camp, and it turned over and spat us out into the water. It was not dangerously deep, and the current didn't wrestle with us. So, Henry and I grabbed our canoe, found floating oars, and directed the canoe to shore.

We then noticed that CF was thrashing in the water, and we were at a loss to know what he was doing. As we got the canoe to shore, we heard him yelling at us to help him. We dashed back into the river and raced to him. The light was poor, but the water about him was all bloody.

It turned out that CF, when thrown into the river, searched for the object that hit the canoe. He first assumed it was a good-sized log, floating near the shore. But when his hand touched the thing in the water, he realized it was not a log. Instead, he knew it was the spirit fish of the river. To catch the great fish was a good omen and an extra blessing from the Great Spirit of the river.

The fish was slow-moving, stunned from hitting the canoe. CF pulled his knife and plunged it into the great fish, which thrashed about. CF pulled his knife from the fish but struggled to wound it again. In a few seconds, he thrust his knife into the giant fish once again. He hung on to the blade with one hand and tried to pull the fish toward shore with the other. His cries for help not only brought Henry and me but also Jacque and Mean Mike, who had already landed on the beach ahead of us.

The five of us forced the great fish to the shore. It was seven feet long and weighed about fifty pounds. We were all shocked at its enormous size and speechless, except for Mike, who shook his head to shed the water in his hair and beard, then said, "It be a fish story nay a soul will believe! Well, done, lad! We need Alf and Dino here to clean and debone this monster."

Henry asked, "What is this huge fish called?"

Jacque said proudly, beaming at CF, "White men call it, sturgeon. It's one of the largest fish. It's a spirit fish, with a toothless mouth and scaleless skin. Mostly, these great ones are about half the length of this one. They can weigh from twenty to one hundred pounds."

CF added, "When young, I hear elders' stories of spirit fish twelve feet long, weight like weaned moose calf. A great gift in the river to us. Saw great fish before. First time, I catch one!"

"We wouldn't have this great gift except for your quick action, CF. You are a great asset to our group," Henry said sincerely. Then Henry, ever a choirmaster, launched into singing, "For he's a jolly good fellow, for he's a jolly good fellow. For he's a jolly good fellow, and so say all of us, so say all of us." Henry realized we had been singing with him and had stopped when he sang, 'and so say all of us.' Henry looked at me and gasped, "Why did you all stop singing?"

"Difference in words, a minor difference. Here, it is most often sung, 'which nobody can deny,'" I said, knowing Henry could be fanatical about song words and tunes.

"It's the American way rather than the British," Mean Mike offered, having heard his Scottish father sing it the British way of Henry.

Henry, always eager for a song, quickly said, "Just a storm in a teacup, for our intents and purposes we'll sing it, which nobody can deny. So, let's toast CF in song!" We did, loudly in good measure, while CF looked at us as those weird White men he was with.

For the next four weeks, life became both hectic and demanding. Two days after the remarkable catch of the sturgeon by CF, Alf and Dino found us. Their boss, Rod Murdock, had fired them. Rod had teamed up with a new partner, a strange southern man with a beautiful but strangely colored hunting dog. The new partner had no respect for Alf and Dino because he felt they could be 'breeds.' However, Rod and the southerner were now partners and heading for Yale. There they were to seal a deal with a mining company as quickly as possible.

Alf and Dino were heading for Yale also but wanted to team up with our group and search for gold. It seemed a good deal for us because they knew the Fraser better than we did, as well as the location of the gravel bars on the way. They liked our approach of checking the bars in case there was gold that was still there. Two extra men would speed up our search for gold on bars without claims. They were willing to have Jacque hold whatever we found and have it split equally at Yale. Alf and Dino would then leave us and hire out as guides to a group of miners once more. The last concern about being our partners was the whole group voting on decisions, to which they agreed.

We received our equal share of gold that had been collected since Smith left us with his share so he could move on. and decided that we would consider if we were finding enough to continue our searching at Yale. Smith had made an impression on us. We needed to determine if we were too relaxed in our prospecting. Did we lack greedy determination, as Smith said?

The addition of the brothers to our partnership was a bumpy adjustment. Alf and Dino were not used to full sunup to sundown days in continuous gold panning or rocker work. As guides, they had freedom to hunt and explore, and they only endured a few hours of gold panning each day. After the first day, they asked to see if they could explore the river to trade for another rocker. They wanted to hunt and take a deer carcass as meat for their trading. We understood how hard it was to keep at the long gold searching, and a rocker did help to spell off the back-bending work of panning.

The brothers were gone hunting before sunrise the following day. We were not sure if they would return, as the daylong gold work had been a challenge to their restless natures. Our work progressed through the day, and we speculated on how Alf and Dino were making out with their hunting and trading. When we returned to camp late in the day, we were delighted at the smell of two rabbits roasting on a spit over coals. A pot of beans was also ready, warming on two stones on the red coals.

The brothers were back in their element. They had traded a deer carcass for two rockers. They could deal with searching for gold when they each had a rocker to work with, as they lacked patience for the gold panning. We were all so impressed with their day of success that Henry led us in a rendition of 'For they are jolly good fellows.' CF joined in with a huge smile, relieved the song was sung at others, not just himself. CF thrived each time someone joined our partnership; he had liked Smith but could sense that he was not at one with us in his attitude. CF felt Alf and Dino were at ease with our group. He said to me, "Seven hearts one now."

The two brothers gave our group great energy and focus. As we slowly made our way toward Yale, our gold searching intensified. We found several gravel bars no longer mined except for some Chinese searching on the sites like ourselves. With three rockers on the go at each location, we could spell off those gold panning. This shorter work at the panning also increased our energy to work the rockers. We were a force to be reckoned with if there was gold; we found it and took it.

The set up and maintaining of our camp were better also. We were content that Alf and Dino were naturals at hunting and fishing, along with CF and Jacque. These four men, working as a brother pair and a father-son pair, alternated days keeping our camp while hunting, fishing, and trading.

Several gravel bars were still fully claimed, with miners open to trading or buying meat or fish. We were able to trade with the Chinese for vegetables, rice, and tea. Our camp often became a place for miners to visit in the evenings for conversation, singing, and music. We did not allow drinking or gambling, as that would have been a great invitation to trouble. Alf, Dino, Jacque, and Henry had the gift of the gab and laughter. Miners were safe visiting us for welcome company and song.

The four traders also spotted miners in need of doctoring and directed them to me. Henry was my assistant. Visitors knew I was not a fully trained or licensed doctor, but I could often help with problems like cuts, infections, pain, and the like. They also knew that I was a preacher but not a thundering type. In chatting with the sick and injured, I was often able to offer the word of God through prayers with them or on their behalf if requested. Discouraged and hopeless men would come in the evening for Bible reading and discussion about God, seeking renewed hope in something greater than gold. They needed someone to listen to them without critical comment on their disappointment, guilt, loneliness, arguments, fights, loss of gold earned to gambling, drinking, opium, and other cares. Only if they asked for a response to their concerns did I offer any.

One such miner was Dutch Daan from Holland. Daan in Dutch meant God is my judge, and Daan came to me crushed with remorse over a fight with another miner. Daan and his partner had a very profitable claim on Hill's Bar in 1858 and gathered tremendous amounts of gold each day. Both became consumed with the wealth they were accumulating. His partner wanted to return to Holland, and he wished to sell his half of the claim to Daan. This need to change their partnership was after seven months of work.

They could not agree on a price for the partner's half of the claim. They got into a pushing match and a fist fight. His partner was bigger and stronger than Daan, and in a rash effort to even the odds when it came to size, Daan hit his partner on the head with his spade. Others saw their fight, and when Daan downed his partner with a hit to his head with his spade, Daan panicked and left his partner there injured on the bar and ran off. He stayed away from the claim for a month. When he returned, he learned that his partner had recovered, sold his share of the claim to someone else, and went back to Holland. The new owner quickly brought in extra help and soon had the whole claim picked clean of gold because Daan was not around. He then left his share of the claim for Daan, knowing it was worthless to him.

After the incident with his partner, Daan had continued searching for gold and had a good stash put away. He wanted to go home to Holland. However, if he went back, he must face his old partner, a family friend who had told Daan's wife that he was dead. His old partner had married his wife to spite him. He could forgive his old partner for stealing his wife as a way of getting even with him. But

Daan could not forgive himself for wounding his partner with his spade and leaving him injured on their claim.

The treatment by a doctor of a cut or rash or broken arm can be very straightforward with satisfactory results. However, helping a man forgive himself and help him believe God forgives him also is no simple task. There are two extremes—those who want no forgiveness from God or anyone else, and those who get stuck on what they have done wrong and cannot get past it.

For Dutch Daan, I reminded him that all sin is against God. His anger was at his partner, and it was his partner that he hit with a spade, but his rage and assault also hurt God. The first thing was to ask God to forgive him for his greed, his argument, his fighting, his striking his opponent with his spade, and for leaving his injured partner. He needed to be sorry to God for his actions. Daan said he would do that. His partner wasn't innocent in their fight, but it was up to his partner to confess his sins against God and Daan.

I suggested that Daan ask God to forgive him not because he deserved forgiveness, but because Jesus died that our sins can be forgiven for His sake. The blood of Jesus purifies us from our sin. Daan said he would also do that.

Lastly, I asked Daan to pray to God, asking Him to show him how he could return to Holland or make a fresh start here in this British Colony. He needed to do what God wanted him to do for not only his own sake but for the sake of the others involved. Daan said he would do that as well.

I felt I could listen to people with a burden of grief or guilt and give suggestions about what could be a Christian answer to their concerns. They could accept or reject my advice as they felt the leading of God. Dutch Daan confessed his sin to God for his actions to his partner. After more soul searching, Daan believed he needed to confess to his old partner his sorrow over his assault against him, so he sent a letter to Holland asking for his forgiveness. I hoped this would help Daan resolve his burden of guilt.

As we worked our way toward Yale, our four traders exchanged things with three different men representing the various groups of Chinese working the gravel sandbars like ourselves. These men wanted to learn more English to talk with White men when searching for gold or to make trade and business deals with the Whites. The three Chinese men would come to our camp a couple of nights a week to learn English words and phrases from Henry and me, to help them in their language skills. CF was eager to take the classes also to see how many White words and phrases he knew or could learn. We used the others in our group to help us teach English to the Chinese. Alf, Dino, and Mean Mike all got a kick out of demonstrating words and phrases and loved being part of the lessons.

One evening we were teaching the Chinese, making sure they became familiar with common English words. Mean Mike was both tall and big as compared to me being short and small. Alf demonstrated how to walk and kept saying the English word 'walk. Dino showed to run. They quickly understood English words common to their lives like river and water, tree, and wood. We would have them tell their recognized English words in phrases and demonstrate them. For example, in English, the Chinese would say 'a big tree' and point out a big tree and say and do the same for a small tree. We were helping them put English words together in a complete way. They had various understanding of a trickle of English words but wanted to grow in their use of the English language.

The English lessons were not usually long, but that evening before the lesson was over, trouble came to visit. First, Lemon Jim, King, Rod Murdock, and Bill Talon arrived in one canoe. Next, a second canoe containing Bow-legged Bill, Old Kelly, Frank Cross, and Jeff Landers followed them to our shore. These last four, plus Bill Talon, were all part of Rod Murdock's workers and well known to Alf and Dino. They landed without an invitation to come ashore. Arrogantly, Rod Murdock demanded to talk to Alf and Dino.

Alf spoke from our group, including the three Chinese men, "What do you want, Murdock?"

"I want to hire you to do some scouting on a river near here." Murdock answered.

"We're not interested!" Dino said for both of them.

"We could drag you two from here by force, but I'd rather you came back to work for me willingly," Murdock both threatened and stated. Tension filled the air, as Murdock wouldn't leave without Alf and Dino, or at least he was trying to intimidate them into thinking he would force them if necessary. Alf and Dino were invaluable guides and the constant source of game and fish to a group they were guiding. No doubt, Murdock was desperate to get them back for the benefit of his group and his new partner. However, the silence from Alf and Dino to Murdock's demands was deafening.

It seemed like the right occasion for me to throw a fit to confuse the enemy and keep them guessing. I began howling, which spurred King into barking. I flung myself to the ground rolled about like a chicken with its head chopped off. Murdock and Lemon Jim and even King the dog were surprised. Jacque and CF began their loud and eerie Indian war cries, and Mean Mike yelled, "Don't leave any of them alive except the dog!"

Henry went running forward at the group, firing two pistol shots in the air. Everyone followed Henry running at Murdock's group except the three Chinese men who stood amazed at the strange events happening before them. Bow-legged Bill, Old Kelly, Frank Cross, and Jeff Landers turned and raced to their canoe, piled in it, and took off. Myself howling and running at them with Alf, Dino, and Jacque catching up with me had impressed upon them that they were not in for a friendly welcome.

Henry ran at Murdock and Lemon Jim, concerned that they might pull pistols and shoot to kill as many of us as they could. Henry did not want to shoot close to the two men, as he might hit King. Bill Talon, Murdock, and Lemon had yelled at King to quit barbing, and that had upset King, who went bounding among the three men not sure which to protect or if all three needed him. The dog's bounding and barbing among them kept Murdock and Lemon from pulling out their pistols.

Henry reached Murdock first and hit him with a solid punch on the chin. Murdock shook his head from the blow but wrestled with Henry for his gun. CF was right behind Henry, and he leaped upon Lemon Jim's shoulders, punching his fists in Lemon's ears, causing the giant to sway on his feet. King was barking and trying to get at CF when Mean Mike arrived and commanded King to sit, which the dog did. As the dog sat, Mike punched Lemon Jim, and his punch sounded like it cracked his fist. Lemon Jim received a double pounding on his ears from CF and crumpled like a mighty oak to the ground.

Bill Talon stood with his hands in the air as a sign of surrender. He was afraid Mean Mike and CF would deal with him next. Jacque had helped Henry subdue Murdock. Alf and Dino announced to Murdock that they would never be his guides again. Understanding his attempted intimidation was over, Murdock and his two companions left quickly. With the aid of Bill Talon, Murdock loaded an unsteady Lemon Jim in their canoe and paddled away with King. Before leaving, Murdock looked at Alf and Dino with enough hate to impress the devil and muttered that they would be sorry for turning their backs on him. Dino fired back at Murdock that anyone foolish enough to work for him could wind up murdered like Smith. That comment brought Lemon Jim alert in the canoe, and we could hear him asking Murdock, "What did he mean by that?" Unfortunately, we couldn't hear Murdock's reply.

The three Chinese men indicated that Murdock and Lemon had traded with them for opium. They offered two English words for the men — 'cheaters' and 'evil.' The trio left having learned the English word 'brawl,' which we had demonstrated for them.

Alf and Dino expressed that they had felt in the dark when we began fighting in response to Murdock's threats. We said they would soon learn that my taking a fit was a signal for war cries and running at the problem, usually just with fists flying. They seemed pretty shocked at our crazy style of fighting. We agreed that we were placing a lot of hope that we could surprise and startle our enemies so we could strike first, and we said we were open to fine tuning our brawling with their suggestions.

CHAPTER TEN:

More Things in Our Favor the Second Time Around

WITH THE ADDITION of Alf and Dino, our progress and success at finding gold increased, and we hoped that it would last until we got to Yale. We did come upon the gravel bar where we had found eight men killed by Natives the previous summer. Their large common grave on the shore seemed to be just as we had left it. A dozen Chinese men were working on the bar, so we went past it. Three of us were thankful to bypass the bar with its history of death. This year it seemed more like a place beside a graveyard rather than a killing site.

We had collected a steady amount of gold since teaming up with Alf and Dino, but it would be split seven ways so that no one person would have great wealth for our arduous work. I prayed it would be a satisfying amount for each of us and cause us to have grateful attitudes.

Dutch Daan approached us as we were getting near to Hill's Bar, close to Yale. He had a partnership offer for our whole group. There was another rich bar across from Hill's Bar called Emory Bar, where he had recently been a partner in a ditching company.

He explained that Emory Bar had also been named Emory and Emory City. When Daan and his partner worked their claim on Hill's Bar in 1858, Emory was a tent and shack mining camp located across from them, on the west side of the Fraser. At that time, the gold findings on Emory Bar seemed to fade quickly and paled in compared to Hill's Bar. The miner's camp at Emory disappeared in about six months.

The current interest in the Emory Bar and Creek area was keen once again because miners were now using flumes and sluice boxes. Until now, Daan never had enough people he trusted to work his claim on Emory Bar with him. Daan's plan was to work this claim, and then return to Holland. He was confident that we would all be more than satisfied with the amount of gold found there. It would be a gamble, either a big failure or a rich success for us all.

Daan was sure he could train us in using his sluice box. He also wanted us to use our three rockers. He understood that we were not familiar with sluicing, but that it was a better method of separating and recovering gold from the gravel using running water. He promised to show us his claim, the water diversion ditch on Emory Creek, examples of flumes, and other sluicing operations so that we could make up our minds for our vote on the matter of partnership with him.

As we reached Hill's Bar and Emory Bar across from it, we decided to set up our camp on the west bank of the Fraser at the mostly uninhabited old miner's camp of Emory. We came upon a lonely, empty miner's shack, so we put our tents beside it. Daan saw our tents and the shack as a mining company that would make us all rich in time. His enthusiasm and vision were contagious, but we needed to consider fully all he had in mind.

Being so close now to Yale, we decided to split our accumulated gold equally, so anyone who wanted to go to Yale could do so for personal supplies and a break from our gold hunting. The next day, Daan showed us what it would mean to partner with him. He led us from our tents nearer to the shore of the Fraser, up the steep climb to where the water was diverted into his big ditch on Emory Creek. Daan made sure to show us everything firsthand. We saw a fast-flowing creek and an extensive irrigation ditch. We looked at flumes made of wood that were tapped into the ditches, dug from the diverted water. We noted that we would be part of a few other mining groups also working with flumes and sluice boxes. We were amazed that the ditches from the diverted water ran both north and south of the junction of Emory Creek and the Fraser River.

Daan was an almost painful potential partner, showing and explaining everything to us in such detail that it was hard not to yawn. He overdid having us see five examples of long and shorter wooden troughs or flumes using gravity to bring water to a miner's digging or a sluice box.

Daan's sluice box was about fifteen feet long and looked like a long open trough that became lower and narrower at one end. Daan went over each detail with us, beginning with how a miner would put a shovel of dirt into the top end and have it wash down the length of the sluice box by the constant flow of water. Gold was caught either by riffles or ridges on the bottom of the sluice box. Overall, it was tedious, but we had to admit that the sluice box worked well with mud and larger chunks of rocks being washed away out the lower end of the box with gold left behind. Daan was so impressed with everything about sluicing that he could only believe that we would be too. We promised Daan that we would think about being in partnership with him and answer him as soon as we were back from Yale.

We spent most of the day with Dutch Daan, so we discussed in general terms our impressions of working with him. As we finished our evening meal, Dino and Alf offered their opinions first.

"I'm finding this gold hunting to be a great adventure, and I'm not in a rush to go back to guiding folks along the Fraser," Dino offered.

"Glad you see it that way, brother," Alf said. "I would also like to have more gold in my pouch before we return to being guides again."

"I'm up to giving it a try," I said, feeling neither great eagerness nor reluctance for a possible new partnership and a new way of searching for gold.

"I feel like I might need to get better boots at Yale, since we will be playing with water troughs," Mike said with a grin.

Jacque said, "I will be okay with this partnership if it isn't for a long time, like many months. I like to keep moving."

Alf and Dino affirmed Jacque's words with, "We feel the same."

CF added to the discussion with an observation that we all seriously considered. He said, "Dutch Daan, like Faro dealer Smith, needs to win. Not one with us."

Henry suggested, "We could set a time limit on our partnership with Daan. A month would be fair to him and us. After that, we can tell better if we want it to go longer. Does that seem reasonable?"

A chorus of yeses came in response to Henry's question. Henry then suggested that we sing a song or two, and he pulled his flute case out and assembled the instrument. We broke into song, and it wasn't long until we were doing our various favorites in full volume. We were amazed when six other miners from around the old Emory campsite joined us, eager to sing. We had thought we had the place to ourselves but began to realize that other miners were also camped in the area. Together the wilderness faded around us. The miners wished us well if we decided to stay and work with Dutch Daan. We felt optimistic about this mostly deserted mining camp of Emory.

It was an exciting day as we set off for our trip to Yale. It was our day off. We had a chance to purchase what we wanted or needed. All of us had a good amount of gold in our pouches as we left, a short trip by canoe. Early in the morning, we set off in three canoes: Henry, CF, and me in one, Jacque and Mean Mike in another, and Alf and Dino in theirs. The other two canoes raced each other to reach Yale first, and Jacque and Mike barely beat out Alf and Dino. Our canoe was last to arrive.

When we disembarked at Yale, CF and Jacque headed for the Hudson's Bay Company fort, and Mike left us to find a barber to shave off his beard. With his beard gone, Mike would look years younger. Mike had his heart set on finding the company of a lady or two after he was looking less like a wild beast. As the weather was moving toward summer heat, Mike also wanted to get his long hair cut to a much cooler length.

Alf and Dino went to look for their contacts that they had for finding people desiring to hire them as guides.

Henry wanted to see what stores and businesses were at Yale before deciding what he wanted to think about purchasing. He and I set off to take in the sights.

I told Henry that while we were at Yale, I had to check in at the fort because Dr. Smith of the Royal Engineers at New Westminster had said that he would contact me through the Hudson's Bay Company forts at Yale or Hope or through Judge Begbie. Dr. Smith wanted me to meet with Dr. John Sebastian Helmcken, a Hudson's Bay Company surgeon, about becoming his assistant. Dr. Smith had been trying to arrange a meeting between us when Dr. Helmcken would be at one of the forts near the gold rush. Dr. Helmcken sometimes trained an assistant, and Dr. Smith wanted me to learn from him if possible. Dr. Helmcken was recognized as one of the most

111

qualified physicians in the colony. He arrived in 1850 at Victoria to work for the Hudson's Bay Company as a surgeon. Then, there was a limited number of people to care for, but that was not the case now, a decade later. Dr. Helmcken, or Dr. John as he was often called, had a home in Victoria but provided medical care to other Hudson's Bay Company posts along the coast and elsewhere.

As we walked about Yale, I shared more about Dr. John because Henry was curious about both the doctor and if I was ready or willing to train as his assistant, to which I could not give an honest answer. Doctoring is such a wondrous calling, but it is so serious and heart stopping on the frontier. It is too often a matter of either life or death, with death at even odds with life.

So, I shared with Henry what Dr. Smith had told me of Dr. John Helmcken. He completed medical school at Guy's Hospital in London, held a license from the Apothecaries Society, and a diploma from the Royal College of Surgeons. I asked Henry, since he is from England, if the doctor's qualifications would be considered excellent there. Henry assured me that they would be exceptional.

Henry was impressed to learn that another of Dr. John's accomplishments was that he was a world traveler. As a young doctor, he journeyed as a ship's physician on voyages to Hudson Bay and India for the Hudson's Bay Company. Henry felt that if the opportunity did arise for me to work as Dr. John's assistant, it would be a terrific learning experience. It would prepare me for medical school in London if I were to go there.

As I finished talking about Dr. John, we came upon a small doorway with a sign over it. In large plain letters, it read, "CONSTABLE." I suggested that we check with him to see if Judge Begbie was in town for a trial or was expected soon for one.

There was one young man behind a desk in the constable's office and an empty jail cell in the corner. The other furnishings in the room were a potbelly stove, three wooden chairs, a boot rack, coat rack, and one great wooden filing cabinet. The young constable was both friendly and smiling.

"Good day, fellows. How can I help you?" he said pleasantly.

"Good day, Constable. We are friends of Judge Begbie, and we are wondering if you might know if he is in Yale or is coming here for a trial soon?" I asked.

"He was here recently, and he left a letter for a fellow. Would you share your names with me?" he asked.

I spoke up, "He knows me as Nothing Brown."

Henry quickly offered, "My name is Henry Arden."

"Would you kindly give your full name, Mr. Arden?" the constable asked Henry.

Henry and I looked at each other, and I said, "I hope it isn't one of his tricks!"

"May as well see what Matthew is up to," Henry sighed and said, "My name, sir, is Henry Sigurd Arden."

"Judge Begbie left an important letter for you from a barrister in England. He charged me with delivering it to you. The English barrister sent it to you in care of Judge Begbie," the constable explained as he offered Henry an official letter from a desk drawer.

"I must have you sign that you got this letter. Judge Begbie needs to notify the barrister that it was received by yourself as a matter of legal proceedings," the constable said. He then produced a paper with a place for the date and a signature that Henry had received the document from Barrister Percy Chester of 9 Dewdney Road, London, England. Henry signed for the letter in deep curiosity but with a particular indication of reluctance.

"You are welcome to take a chair and sit to read your letter," the constable offered Henry.

I realized Henry might want to consider his letter in private, and I said to him, "Sounds like a promising idea. Sit and read your letter, and I will wait for you outside." I left the office quickly so Henry could deal with his letter. Following my lead, the constable said, "I'll be just outside. I could use some fresh air."

We stood together outside the office while Henry read the contents of the document. The constable shared that he liked Judge Begbie and was pleased to meet us, as he had heard positive things about us from him. In passing the time with small talk, I asked him about the occurrence of crime in Yale. The constable said that there was more than enough to keep five constables busy. Then he shared that earlier in the week, a man with a bluetick coonhound dog was found dead, shot in the back. No one was a friend or associate of the dead man, but there was tremendous interest in the coonhound. The chief constable was going to auction off the dog later that afternoon to pay for the cost of a plot and the burial of the murdered man. I would have asked more about the auction, but Henry came out of the office looking calm and thanked the constable for his help and kindness.

I asked the constable quickly, "Where will the auction of the dog be held, and at what time?"

He said, "Here, outside the office, at three this afternoon."

I said to Henry, "If you are okay, we need to find Mean Mike as fast as possible, as he will want to bid on the bluetick coonhound. It sounds like it is Lemon Jim's dog, King. Lemon was murdered earlier this week."

Henry replied, "Lemon must be dead as a doornail, for he would never sell King if he were alive. Yes, let's get to Mean Mike before he has spent all his gold."

I steered us to the Hudson's Bay Company post, hoping to find Jacque and CF. They were still there and about to order their supplies. We excitedly explained we needed to find Mean Mike so that he could bid on the bluetick dog.

An employee at the fort directed Jacque to the three most popular houses of the prettiest ladies, where Mike might be visiting. Jacque and CF set off to see if Mike was at one of them. If they couldn't find him, then they would begin saloon searching. Henry and I headed for the barbershop in case Mike was still there, and then we would hunt the bars and gambling places, as Mike had wanted to see if he could win at Faro.

We had no luck finding Mean Mike at the barbershop, but we did run across Alf and Dino, who volunteered to keep a lookout for Mike and direct him to the auction if they saw him. We did not find Mike at any gambling places either. Eventually, we ran into CF and Jacque, who had not found him either. It was noon, and there was a plain, modest-looking café with a sign that read: "Kelly's Café, Tasty Food at a Cheap Price. Stay out if you have no manners." The sign made us smile, and we imagined Kelly to be a lady of considerable size and force or a tough Irishman ready to throw out rude customers.

We were surprised when CF said, "This place, Mike eat." Henry replied, "Well, let's see." We entered the busy café, where there was not an empty table to sit at. A beautiful, petite, lady, not over five feet tall, greeted us with a coffee pot in her right hand.

She said in a charming Scottish accent, "Hi, I'm Kelly. It won't be long, gentlemen, until a table is ready for you. Please have a seat on the bench near the window. We will call you as soon as we can."

We decided to sit and wait while looking for Mike among the people eating there. We were hardly seated when Mean Mike appeared from the kitchen, carrying plates of food, and delivering it to a table. We barely recognized him with his beard gone and his hair cut. Mike blushed red and lumbered over to us.

He blurted out to us, as if it was an important secret, "I'm in love. That Maggie Kelly who owns this place be the prettiest lassie in the world. I walked by here after I got my hair cut, and she was sweeping the street in front of this here café. I told her that she was the prettiest lassie I've ever seen."

"What did she say to that?" Henry asked Mike for all of us.

"She said to me, 'I think you're too tall. But I detect ye may be a fool or a jackass who goes about flattering a lady you've never met before.' I tell you lads, I just stood there, my mouth open without a word to answer her. Finally, I stammered out, 'Anyone would be a fool or a jackass not to see you as a beautiful angel and tell you so.'"

I asked, "So what did she say to that?"

Mike gushed on, "She said, 'I have no time for sweet talking men. No man will win my heart by empty words. You'd need to be ready to work as hard or harder than I do in the kitchen. So, take yourself on down the street, and charm someone else.' So, I told her, 'I'll work as hard as you, as a kitchen is no threat to me.' Then she responded, 'No man has ever wanted to work beside me in my café, but I doubt you can work hard enough to win even a smile from me.'"

As his words were hardly out of Mike's mouth, Maggie Kelly appeared to tell Mike that meals in the kitchen were ready for customers, and he should get them out hot. She gave us a smile and said, "I think he has the makings of a decent husband, but I have neither the patience nor desire for one."

She disappeared as quickly as she had appeared, and the four of us were too amazed to speak. The shock of it all had hardly worn off when Maggie showed us to a table. I asked her if we could please speak to Mike, as it was an urgent matter.

She said, "I'll send him out when I take your order to the kitchen. You look like you all want the special today, so it'll be four specials coming up." She was gone before we could object, but we acted like what she said was just dandy with us.

In a brief time, Mike appeared, and he asked with a grin, "Lads, what urgent business do you have with me? I'm busy winning the heart of this beautiful lady, who is very resistant to my charm."

Henry said, "Mike, it seems Lemon Jim is dead, and his dog, King, will be auctioned off at three today before the constable's office. If you're too busy with the lady, give me your gold pouch, and I'll buy him for you."

Mike turned without a word and went back to the kitchen. We looked at each other in amazement.

Jacque said, "Hard choice between a lovely woman and a highly prized dog. We'll see if Mike can get both of them." His comment led to a discussion of how King was already well trained, but it might take a heap more than patience to train Mean Mike as a husband.

Mean Mike and Maggie returned, carrying plates ladened with food. Mike was going to eat with us, as he had a plate for himself. Maggie said to us with a slight grin, "I'm returning this fellow to your care. He's got his heart set on a bluetick hound dog. Seems that he has so quickly forgotten that I'm the prettiest lass in the world, according to him." She then looked directly at Mike and said, "You better leave a good tip." Then she looked back at us and exclaimed, "Eat up fellows, while the food is hot," and she was gone.

Each platter came with a large, thick slice of fried ham, two large sausages, three pancakes with syrup, a heap of fried potatoes, and a thick slice of bread and butter. We devoured the food before us, while Maggie poured us each a cup of strong black coffee. During the meal, Mike explained that he had great fun helping Maggie and showing her that he was not without talents in a kitchen. His mother had enlisted him to help her cook, as there were thirteen children to feed, and Mike was the oldest of them. Mike also told us that he had only spent a little of his gold on a shave and haircut, and he was visibly excited that he might own King. We were all hopeful for

Mike's success at buying the dog, and we voted at the table to accept the dog into our partnership if he did acquire him.

After lunch, most of us had supplies to get at the fort and elsewhere, so we all gathered what we wanted and were at the constable's office by three. There were about a dozen men interested in the dog. Mike and Henry knew King best, and they were sure it was the dog Lemon Jim was so proud of possessing. The chief constable was punctual and made it clear that payment would need to be immediate upon the conclusion of the auction. Mike had changed some of his gold for money in case he needed to pay for the dog. The bidding was slow and low at first, but it soon became apparent that two other men besides Mike wanted the dog and seemed willing to pay dearly for him.

The constable halted the auction and said, "The bidding now stands at the cost of the plot and burial for the dog's owner." He handed Mike and the other two men a small slip of paper and a pencil. He asked, "Is there anyone else wanting to make a final bid on the bluetick coonhound?" No one indicated that they did. He announced, "The bid is now at five dollars, so for the three of you, write down how many more dollars you would pay for the dog as your final bid." Each man wrote on their slip of paper and folded it in half. The constable asked the men to come forward and open their slip of paper for himself and everyone to see. The first man had written two dollars so the constable said, "You would pay seven dollars." The second man had written four dollars, so the constable said, "Your final bid is nine dollars." Mike had written seven dollars, and the constable said, "Your final bid is twelve dollars. The dog goes to you."

Mike was pleased to be the owner of King, and we shared his joy as our own. Mike was paying the constable when Maggie Kelly appeared. She stepped up to Mike and said, "The dog is beautiful. Bring him to the café, as I have scraps and a beef bone for him."

Mike smiled at Maggie and said, "That's mighty kind of you, but it will cost you kiss."

Maggie Kelly looked at us and said, "I told you this Mike guy is forward, and now you see he lacks any common sense, as he is willing to pay twelve dollars for a hound. I've told him I'm not looking for a husband, especially one with a dog, but he is too dense to understand. I'll send him running back to your gold camp once I feed his dog. He won't be long." She grabbed Mike by the arm and said, "Come on, let's get this fine dog fed before I change my mind." We watched them go down the street, King close to Mike's one side and Maggie on the other.

CHAPTER ELEVEN:
Staying Put and Content

FIRST TO ARRIVE back at camp, Alf and Dino started supper, as they figured everyone would be returning early evening if Mike was able to buy King. When we got there, Henry was intent on brewing a pot of coffee for everyone to celebrate the arrival of King, so he stayed with Alf. CF and me decided to gather firewood while waiting for Mike and Jacque to get back to camp with King. As we went along, CF alerted me that we were not alone on our chore, and he signaled me to stay still. He carefully put his armful of wood down, and then went ahead on his own to check out what he thought he heard. Moving along noiselessly, CF came to a clearing, where he found Dutch Daan talking with . . . Lemon Jim. He stayed concealed to listen to them talk because Lemon Jim was supposedly dead.

Dutch Daan said, "I told you not to trust Rod Murdock, but shooting him in the back could provoke your hanging by the British, who you despise."

"I don't need or want your opinion. I have all the contracts and agreements for gold that I want. As soon as you pay me for my share in the irrigation ditch, I'll be gone," Lemon Jim barked at Daan.

"I told you that I'll have the money for you tomorrow. Meet me here at dawn, and I'll have the money then. I want to start sluicing early, so don't be late," Dutch Daan told Lemon.

"I think you're stalling me," Lemon said, pulling out a pistol. "I shot Murdock in the back. Maybe I'll shoot you in the gut, Dutchman," Lemon threatened.

"Go ahead and shoot me because I don't have the money on me and if I am dead, you still won't get it," Daan dared him.

Lemon did not lower his gun and kept it pointed at Dutch Daan. CF arose out of hiding and said calmly but forcefully, "Think, Lemon. Dutch Daan no alone. Put gun away and go!"

Totally surprised to see CF and unwilling to press his threat further in case there were more men with him, Lemon said, "I'll be here at dawn for my money." He backed out of the clearing with the pistol still in his hand.

"Thank you, CF. I never trusted Rod Murdock, but Lemon Jim now seems even worse than him. He is capable of murder. I think he might have shot me even though I said that I didn't have any money on me. A damn disturbing thought!"

"Glad he no shoot you, new boss," CF said with a smile.

"I hope I'm your new boss. Can I come to your camp?" Daan asked.

"Sure. You help bring firewood," CF said and led Daan back to me.

I was surprised to see Daan, but CF said, "Dutch Daan come to our camp. Him bring firewood too."

"I think supper should be about ready when we get there, so Daan, I'm inviting you to eat with us," I said to him.

"Sounds good to me," Daan answered.

We might have talked more, but we could hear barking coming from the direction of our camp. I said to Daan, "There is big excitement. There was a man found dead at Yale last week, by the name of Lemon Jim. Someone shot him in the back, and they auctioned off his beautiful bluetick coonhound to pay for the man's funeral and gravesite. Mike bid on the dog and purchased it."

"That's pretty exciting alright," Dutch Daan said, looking at CF. Then he added, "There is a little more about Lemon's death that I'll share at camp, as I believe we are almost there."

I hardly got out the words "You're right," when King came bounding up to us at a fast run, briefly circled us, and then headed back to camp.

Reaching camp, we found an atmosphere of joy and laughter at King's racing and barking. The dog was enjoying his freedom and exercise. When he began to slow down, Mean Mike felt he'd had enough exercise and commanded him to sit, which the dog did obediently.

Everyone at camp welcomed Dutch Daan, and Alf and Dino assured him there was plenty of food for him to join us for supper. As we ate, Mike gave King a big beef bone to chew on that had been provided by Miss Kelly. King seemed content beside Mike and gave the bone his serious attention. It was evident that King remembered both Mike and Henry kindly, and he didn't seem to be offended with any of the rest of us, at this his welcome party. Our metal plates were filled and emptied of beans with bacon. Fine fresh baked bread from Yale with the treat of butter made the meal extra special. Not only had Henry bought coffee, some of which he had brewed for the finish of our meal, but he also produced two store-bought round pound cakes, so everyone could have cake for dessert.

When the cakes had vanished into our stomachs and we had drained the coffee from our tin cups, Dutch Daan asked if we could hold our vote so he would know if we would become his partners in sluicing for gold. Before we could answer, Alf and Dino announced they would be leaving us.

Dino spoke first, saying, "We had every intention of staying with you men longer, but a mining company team met with us in Yale. There is big interest in all the reports of the finding of gold beyond the Fraser, and these company men are willing to pay us well to guide them to check out the various reported gold strikes. They want to mine below ground for gold or silver in a serious way and buy up mining claims in the places with the best prospects for gold. Tell them where we are guiding the two men first, Alf."

"Well, the initial place we are to guide them to is Rock Cliff. It is just the first on the list of sites that they want to visit without delay. It is near the boundary between this colony and the United States. The gold rush there was sparked off last year when two American soldiers were being chased by Indians, and they crossed the boundary to escape their pursuers. The two soldiers found gold on the banks of the Kettle River, where it meets Rock Creek. This year, the first claim has been filed, and the race is on to find gold there. Many Americans and a number of Chinese are swarming to Rock Creek, and a town is developing there as I speak. Dino, tell them some of the other places that gold has been found that the two mining officials also want to investigate."

"Fellows, last year gold was discovered at Harper's Camp on a river they call, Horsefly River. It is a gold strike between the Cariboo Mountains and Quesnel Lake. It's another place we are to guide the men to. There is something else the men want to check out. The miners following the Fraser River have been searching the Quesnel River, a major tributary of it. The Cariboo mountains, as well as the Quesnel River and Cariboo River, are where gold is being found now. Where the Quesnel River and Cariboo meet is called the Forks, and gold was also found there last year. As of this very month, there are rumors of more discoveries near the Forks at Keithley and Antler

Creeks. Listen guys, you cannot believe gold strike talk, but the two mining officials have word that the gold is so close to the surface of Antler Creek that there is no need to dig for it. I doubt it, but they say that you can get seventy-five to one hundred dollars' worth of gold in a single gold pan," Dino said with such excitement that he was almost shouting as he finished.

We were all listening in surprise and amazement to everything the two brothers were sharing with us. There were a few seconds of total silence when Dino stopped speaking. "It's easy to see your eagerness to guide the mining officials. I wish you mates well, and I will find it hard to replace your excellent voices for singing," Henry said, breaking the lull.

I spoke next, "I, we, all wish you safe travels and know the two mining officials will be lucky to have you as their guides." The rest of the group nodded their agreement.

Dutch Daan asked, "Now that Alf and Dino are leaving, will the five of you who are left go into a sluicing partnership with me?" His voice betrayed a seriousness and a hint of apprehension.

"Do we need to discuss it together? Or do we just say yes or no now?" I asked.

"Let's just decide now," Jacque exclaimed. "I say yes."

Henry let out a "Me too," and myself, Mean Mike, and CF repeated it.

I looked at Dutch Daan and said, "Now it is official. We are your partners. So, repeat once again the terms of our arrangement, as we start work tomorrow. We trust Alf and Dino and are fine with them hearing our agreement. If you are okay with that, state how this deal is to work for all of us."

Dutch Daan began to outline the partnership. "We agree that it is to last thirty days starting tomorrow. At the end of thirty days, we will know if we are finding gold and how much. If we are willing, we can go another thirty days. I will be working largely at the large irrigation ditch and checking on those using its water for their mining operations." Dutch Daan paused to slap a hungry mosquito, as the later evening was swarming with them.

Daan said that he would try to talk faster so we could soon escape the mosquitoes. He continued like a boss, "At the end of each day, I will meet with Jacque, who I trust with the gold collected, as you also do. He and I will split the gold in half daily. He will give you your shares as you decide among yourselves. I would like Jacque to oversee the sluice box and the three rockers. I will train him first, and then he will train you. I need three of you there with Jacque each day, and one of you can look for food and take care of the camp. It will be sunup to sunset each day. Before we start tomorrow, there is one complication for you to consider. I'll let CF tell you what he saw before supper tonight."

"Me saw Lemon Jim talking to Daan. Lemon want to shoot Daan. I say to Lemon, 'Daan no alone.' Lemon leave with his gun," CF told us.

Mean Mike said, "Alive or not, I'll not give King back to Lemon."

Dutch Daan said, "Yes, Lemon Jim is alive, wanting money from me, as I'm buying his part in the cost of the irrigation ditch here on

Emory Creek. He was to collect his money tomorrow, but he demanded it tonight. I told him that I did not have his money, and he would get it tomorrow. Lemon wasn't going to wait until then. He claimed that he shot Rod Murdock in the back, and he was threatening to shoot me until CF made his presence known."

Alf and Dino both chimed in, "Lemon didn't shoot Rod Murdock in the back." Dino finished saying on his own, "Because we saw Rod Murdock at Yale today. He was boarding a steamer. He saw us and muttered a curse at us."

"Well, who be the man found dead in Yale? Why was King found with the dead man?" Mean Mike questioned aloud.

"It could be the man was a victim of a scam by Lemon Jim and Rod Murdock. I did not realize I was getting tied up with double-crossing, crooked devils when I did business with Lemon Jim through his agent Rod Murdock."

"Neither did we when we signed on as guides for Rod Murdock. Everything with Murdock is a sham, so he can rip-off or murder as he goes along," Alf affirmed.

"Daan, keep going with your story, my brother can't hold his tongue when there is mention of Rod Murdock," Dino proclaimed.

Daan continued, "Rod contacted me because they had been checking out mining claims for sale on Hill's Bar and learned these were more in demand on Emory's Bar. Murdock heard that me and another man had been working on a water diversion ditch on Emory Creek and insisted that his partner would want to be included in such an ownership, where miners would pay for water rights to their claims. We told them we were not interested in any investment from them. As we were almost done the ditch, my partner became sick and insisted on selling his share of the ditch ownership to me. My partner was becoming sicker and sicker each day and needed to return home while he could. I bought him out, and he took a steamer to Victoria on his way home to California." Daan paused to swat away mosquitoes, who seemed to have a persistent taste for his Dutch blood.

"Seems strange that your partner started to get sicker and sicker. Do you have any idea what was ailing him?" Henry asked.

"As a matter of fact, I do." Daan answered. He explained, "At the time, I didn't realize he was being poisoned by Murdock so he would sell. When my partner Red got to Victoria, he went to see a doctor who was said to be one of the best in the colony, Dr. John. The physician observed him and his symptoms and said it sounded like arsenic poisoning, the effects of which would gradually wear off. My partner did begin to feel better, but he still decided to return to his home in California. He sent word to warn me about Murdock and Lemon, as one of them would often eat with him at Yale. They were generous, often buying his meals."

I could not help myself, and I blurted out, "Arsenic poisoning is an age-old art that is called the widow maker of wealthy husbands."

"Well, it is an art that Murdock and Lemon use to get what they want. Murdock or Lemon were poisoning my partner's food to upset our partnership. I say that because once my partner was gone, things began to go wrong at the irrigation ditch; vandalism, and I needed to post a guard day and night. Four miners ready to get water rights from the ditch backed out. I have much of my money invested in this ditch and was struggling so that I would not lose everything."

Jacque spoke out this time, "So when you were in a fix, the two skunks Rod and Jim came along to rip you off if they could."

"Yes," Daan said in a tired voice, "Rod Murdock and Lemon Jim came along, wanting to still invest in the ditch. I was ready to begin working my claim but needed to hire workers and place my own ditch and flume. I took money from Lemon Jim for a quarter ownership. I can report to you that the workers on my claim found a good amount of gold, which I tried to keep secret from Murdock and Lemon, but I discovered that two of the workers were pocketing much of the gold they found and reporting to their boss, Rod Murdock."

"There is no honest dealing with a crooked man, and the worst of crooks run in pairs or packs," Henry announced.

"That is the God's truth," Daan said as he continued, "I confronted Murdock and told him to keep away from my irrigation ditch and my claim. Which he did, but Lemon began demanding more money from his quarter share. So, I told him I would buy out his share, and we agreed on tomorrow for his payment, yet he showed up today. But there is one other thing I found out about Lemon Jim, he has sold King many times, and then managed to steal King away from his new owner to sell the dog again to another person. I suspect that may explain the dead body at Yale."

"Are you saying that the dead man might have been someone who bought King, and then caught Lemon Jim or Murdock trying to steal the dog back from him?" Mike asked Dutch Daan.

"Maybe. There is a connection to King. For whatever reason, the coonhound seemed to have stayed with the man shot in the back. Maybe he did not die quickly, and King remained. If Lemon Jim knows you have King, he'll be waiting to steal the dog from you," Daan stated.

"I think you be right in that," Mike said, petting King.

"Lemon want money. Might kill Daan dawn tomorrow. We protect Daan," CF announced.

"CF is right. Don't meet Lemon Jim without us being there," Henry said to Dutch Daan.

"Thank you. That is a promising idea. Lemon Jim and Rod Murdock are snakes who keep hidden and are always ready to strike. We all need to be watchful because they know my claim is rich in gold. Everyone should be around when Henry and I split any gold collected because Lemon and Murdock are animals in heat for the treasure," Daan said.

Dutch Daan soon bid us good night and said he would meet us in our camp at dawn and have us accompany him to meet Lemon Jim.

Alf and Dino asked how far away Daan's camp was located, and he said that it was near his irrigation ditch. They said they would pack up and take him there, then leave from there in the morning. . We were genuinely sad to see Alf and Dino go but glad they would be Dutch Daan's protection until dawn.

After the three men left, we discussed that Dutch Daan should make his camp with us as of tomorrow. This was a new reality starting for us, working under a boss, learning a new way of getting gold, and having a dog in camp and at work with us. I for one did not like the idea that we must watch our backs for Lemon and Murdock. Frenchy and his brothers already had a way of showing up and annoying us.

I suggested when we were ready to go to our tents that King should have the old shack as his doghouse. I also told Mike that he should tie the dog up at night so he would not wander off.

Mean Mike looked at me and said, "Too late, Nothing. I already have water and his beef bone in the shack, and a rope for his collar that stretches to my tent."

"I should have known you had everything thought out. Have a good night, Mike, and you too, King!" I said as I went to our tent. I slept despite concerns about the meeting between Daan and Lemon Jim the next morning and the first day of our partnership starting. Henry, me, and CF were up at dawn, drinking Jacque's black tea.

Jacque told us, "As soon as you three were in your tent, Mike had King beside him in ours. I may have to get my own tent or move to the shack doghouse. Mike and King are off on a walk in the woods, which should awaken every animal there."

"I heard ye," Mike said, returning with King. "Give me your witch's brew, and let's eat our gluey porridge before Daan arrives." As we finished our breakfast, Dutch Daan came to our camp. We insisted he drink a cup of tea, which would make a man of him if he could stomach it. Daan drank the hot black tea like it was chilly water and said it wasn't strong enough for a Dutchman.

CF and Daan led the way to the meeting with Lemon Jim in the clearing. They were well ahead of us, so it was just the two of them. Me, Henry, and Jacque followed close enough to keep Daan and CF in view but spread out. We hung back out of sight as best we could.

Mike kept King and himself well back from us, as he didn't want Lemon Jim to see King. Henry was trying to get close to the clearing so that he could help out if needed.

When they reached the open expanse, Dutch Daan and CF stopped short when they saw Lemon Jim standing with a grin, Rod Murdock and Bill Talon beside him.

"I thought you might have your men with you, so I brought my business partner and his bodyguard," Lemon Jim said, "I hope you have brought my money at last."

"I have it, and I'm sure you will want to count it. CF will give it to you," Dutch Daan said and nodded to the young man, who walked over to give Lemon Jim the package.

"Don't give it to me. That's why my business partner is here. Give the money to him, fool." Lemon Jim said in a voice that sounded like he was becoming unglued in his head. When CF gave it to Murdock, Lemon screamed at Murdock, "Count it! Now!"

It took Murdock a long time to count it. When he was done, he said, "There's five hundred here."

Dutch Daan startled us as he shouted like he too was a half a foot from madness. "Count it again. It is all there!"

Daan's shout brought Frenchy and his two brothers rushing into the clearing. Frenchy yelled at Lemon Jim, "Just kill them. We are ready to work his claim and take care of water rights on the ditch."

CF broke into a loud, scornful laugh at Frenchy, and he said to Lemon Jim, "I shoot him in ass with arrow. He scream like baby. His brothers run away like rabbits." Effortlessly, CF jumped high in the air and quickly landed with a flip in front of Frenchy and his brothers, a knife in his hand, causing them to back up out of reach. "Cowards!" CF yelled in their faces, and then turned and ran at Bill, Murdock, and Lemon Jim, the men scrambling back to avoid CF's knife blade.

Frenchy and his brothers exploded in French curses and ran after CF. With the men in his pursuit lunging to grab him, CF dodged behind

Murdock. Luckily for CF, Frenchy and his brothers crashed into Murdock, sending the package of money flying in the air. One of Frenchy's brothers grabbed the parcel, and the trio ran off with the money.

They got away because CF pushed Bill Talon into Murdock, who was getting up from being hit by Frenchy and his brothers. Jacque had appeared unnoticed and had a pistol pointed at Murdock and Talon, who decided to stay still as Jacque suggested. When CF confronted Frenchy, they took off after him.

Dutch Daan, a big man himself, slugged Lemon Jim, who yelled, "You can't hit me!" Daan slugged him again, saying, "Yes, I can." They might have yelled and punched longer at each other, but Henry fired a shot in the air and shouted, "Hold it," to Daan and Lemon.

Dutch Daan said, "Get your money from Frenchy and his brothers. Get out of here! Don't come back or go near my claim or ditch. I have already reported you to the constable at Yale for threatening me with a gun yesterday, Lemon."

"The constable knows that I'm dead, so he would not have listened to you," Lemon said.

Henry spoke up, "The constable knows that Dutch Daan is our partner and that he can be trusted. We are recommended to the constable by Judge Begbie.

"So, you say," Lemon Jim replied skeptically, but he, Murdock, and Bill Talon left, and we escorted them until they were in a canoe and paddling away from Emory on the Fraser.

Once again, we were all impressed by the bravery and quick action of CF, and we congratulated him. Even Dutch Daan, a gruff man devoid of emotion, said to CF, "Thank you!" and gave him a bear hug. When Dutch Daan let go of the hug, he turned red, then muttered, "We got a lot of work to get to before the day is over." With that, he led us to work. For the first two days, Daan wanted the five us to learn his demands. From the third day on, usually CF or Mike guarded camp, hunted, or fished, and prepared food.

Being under the direction of Dutch Daan was a rude awakening for us. We were accustomed to a relaxed way of working together, allowing each other to move at a comfortable pace. Daan saw us as a cog in the wheel of the production of gold. On the job, Daan was only concerned about what each of us were doing and doing it right. He did not want us questioning his methods or giving our opinions. Getting gold was Daan's motivation, and it was obvious we were necessary to him as long as we did what he expected.

At supper, we were looking at each other thinking what did we get ourselves into with this mad Dutchman?

Mean Mike broke the damn of pent-up feelings from our first day. He said with pure gloominess, "I felt I was back dealing with my fault-finding old man in his blacksmith shop. Lads, I hate when someone's looking for me to make a mistake so they can correct me."

Henry muttered, "None of us has any identity as a person in Daan's eyes. When you work for him, you owe him your body, soul, and mind."

"This sluicing may give more gold, but it has to be further panned and washed, and maybe even screened. It seemed to be extra drudgery to me. I will need Mike's jokes or some singing to keep me from taking a fit from boredom," I confessed.

"Boss-man want quiet. Hard to do all day. Maybe we give Daan to Lemon Jim," CF added.

CF's suggestion resulted in cheering and clapping from the rest of us.

Henry said what we were all thinking, "Our first day would suggest we may not be here long."

Little did we realize, our partnership with Daan would last in spite of our first day of work together. It would teach us the dark side of gold and the cost of chasing dreams.

Our boss was firm but fair to his workers. He was hard working without mercy on himself, determined to have his claim worked well, and his irrigation ditch managed perfectly. We as a group said that Daan was ambitious to the point of insanity. We could feel his powerful need to succeed on the very first day of our partnership. In a sense, he was like Smith, always planning ahead and counting what had the best chance of succeeding. Our partnership, although rocky at first, worked over time, as Dutch Daan learned to accept us as individuals without comparing or judging us for what were our limits.

We discovered that Daan actually wanted us to learn and keep learning, admit problems and mistakes, and to not ever give up. He was impressed from our first day that we did not blame each other even if there was reason and that we trusted each as brothers. Dutch Daan learned that if he had a problem with one of us, he had a problem with all of us. He would come to see that we were loyal to each other and to him as our boss. He had to deal with us with respect, and not as a boss ordering his workers around.

It took a while for Daan to understand that although we were often singing, laughing, or talking as we worked, we were not neglectful or negligent of our duties. Gradually, he understood that our gold search was an adventure and fellowship of friendship and respect for life. We were neither lazy nor indifferent to the value of gold, however, individually and as a group, we refused to be driven to get more and more. We understood searching for gold was a temporary venture in our lives. We hoped that when we were done, we had some gold to show for our efforts, but the most important thing was coming out alive. As our partnership bloomed, Dutch Daan understood that he could trust us because were not out for every speck of gold we could get.

Dutch Daan had enjoyed success on Hill's Bar and knew the danger of getting a substantial amount of gold. He told us on the first day, "The more gold you gain, the more it may destroy you and others."

At first, we did not take his warnings seriously but as the days went on, we realized we were each accumulating gold. Now we had to think about more than one gold pouch. For each of us to have a full pouch of gold and to be starting on a second was both exciting and nerve-racking. We were each receiving gold more often and needed to store it somewhere or carry it on our bodies at all times. Carrying gold at all times was a positive necessity, as well as a strange burden and distraction. I could no longer say, "I don't have enough gold to worry about."

Being close to Yale, there was the concern that no one of us should appear to have more than a little gold in public when buying supplies, at a saloon, or at the assayer's office. Life became complicated, gold began to control us. We had more wealth, but we needed to spend only a little of it at any one time. It was hardest for Mean Mike, who wanted to gamble freely, drink the expensive whiskey, and impress the lovely Miss Kelly. Mike said, "I had more fun when I was almost broke."

CHAPTER TWELVE:
Days of Bleakness

WE WERE LIVING proof that nightmares did come true. Working under Dutch Daan was an assault on our characters. We were meeting a success at getting gold that was impressive and sobering, but we were under work pressures we had never faced before. We were stretched each day physically, as we were hard-pressed to work at the pace and dedication that Daan insisted. Finally, the morning of the third week, Mother Nature helped us in mellowing Dutch Daan's demand to work at his unremitting rate.

A week of relentless rain resulted in very muddy and challenging work conditions. Mike told Daan, "There's been a shifting of the flume's incline on the slope of the land to the sluice box, and it looks like it will slide or slip downward. So, with all the rain we have had, I don't think it is a good idea to release more water into the flume, as you're planning to do."

"I'll shore up the flume if it needs it before I release more water into it."

Henry questioned Daan, "It is so muddy, and it is pouring rain again. Could we leave the sluicing until this afternoon and hopefully by then, the rain will be less troublesome?"

"Pouring rain and mud are part of sluicing. There is no gold to be found sitting in a dry camp," Dutch Daan muttered in anger.

We were all surprised by Henry, who said, "You, sir, are inviting accidents and injury. If the flume slides down the slope, will you catch it, or will you expect us to do so? Do you want us to pick up your sluice box and hold it over our heads so the flume can slide by it?"

"Enough," Dutch Daan bellowed. "The flume can take the extra water, and it will stay in place. I will make sure of it." So off Daan went up the incline, slipping in the mud and wet rocks. He got down on his muddy knees at the bottom of the flume to check the log and rocks that anchored it in place. His poking at them to ensure they were secure caused them to slide out in a rush of mud and water. The flume moved on top of Dutch Daan's arm and shoulder, and he cursed in pain, sending us up the hill to help him. Thankfully, the mud cushioned his arm and shoulder, so they weren't broken but pinched and caught under the flume. We could not move the flume off Daan until Mike got the water gate to the flume closed. After that, the flume empty of water was a bit more manageable in its weight.

Dutch Daan remained alert although in great pain. He was in shock but able to walk with Mean Mike holding on to his good arm. The flume slid down the incline five feet as we walked Dutch Daan back to our camp. Daan could move his arm and shoulder, but they were both painful, scraped, and bruised.

When we reached our camp, Daan could not believe that we had filled the holes in the roof of the old, deserted shack. We had taken down the front side of the hut completely, using the boards to patch the roof. The shack was now three-sided with a rough board table in it, which we had constructed from the remainder of the front wall. This dwelling was a place to cook out of the rain. It was stacked with firewood along the back wall and had a fire pit near the open side.

We had found an old wooden barrel that we patched to collect rainwater for washing and cooking, and we placed it near the front entrance of the shack. Dutch Daan remained in a daze, and we got him out of his muddy clothes and cleaned up. I tended to his bruised and scraped arm and shoulder. Jacque brought in his bedroll and blanket, and we had Dutch Daan stretch out in the shack near the fire. We were drenched from work. The rain poured on, so we huddled in the shack, both wet and muddy. Henry couldn't stand himself being soaking wet and muddy, so he stretched a rope between two trees and hung his muddy wet clothes to wash in the pouring rain. He hung Dutch Dan's sodden garments also.

When Henry returned to the shack in his soaking wet underwear and said he'd hang our wet and muddy clothes on the line for a wash in the rain, his demand to wash our clothes seemed crazy. Still, we all said thanks and gave them to him.

Jacque made his awful black tea to drink, which was quickly consumed in genuine appreciation. Dutch Daan awoke soon after, sat up, had a drink of tea, and then asked, "Where are my clothes?"

Henry said, "They're in the wash!" Dutch Daan stared at us all in our underwear and looked confused, then laid down and went back to sleep.

I was afraid for Henry's mental state that day, for after he drank his tea, he disappeared to our tent and returned almost immediately with his ironing board and iron. He placed the iron in the fire to heat up.

CF whispered to me, "I think Henry needs help, him acting like a demon spirit in his head."

"We are all feeling like we do not fit here in this sluicing, and Henry can't stand mud and dirty clothes. He is from a world of clean apparel and clean hands, and this is his way of seeking a bit of control in a place he hates. He needs us to help him with that," I explained.

"You do what want, and I follow you," CF whispered to me.

I announced loudly, "CF is going to help Henry iron the clothes dry when they are ready. Mike, I need your help to wring out the wet garments. Jacque, would you please make a soup or stew for a meal while we do this?"

Jacque nodded.

Mike gladly came out in the rain to help me take down and wring out Henry's wet clothes. He said, "Henry is close to exploding. I hope he don't brand Dutch Daan with his hot iron."

"These days of rain and extra mud have pushed him over the edge. We all feel we are drowning up to our necks in work beyond our control or input. None of us are quitters, but it may be hardest for Henry to cope with dealing with a demanding boss, as well as the mud, which he hates," I said.

Henry's clothes were relatively clean from the pouring rain, but we rinsed them in the water barrel, and the mud was gone. Mike was able to wring them out with his big, powerful hands. We gave them to Henry, who set about ironing them. Shortly, Henry was wearing his mostly dry clothes, and CF began ironing Dutch Dan's, so they would be ready for him when he awoke. Mean Mike and I got skilled at getting the clothes off the rope and giving them a final rinse in the rain barrel. Mike wrung out the garments like he was a mad strangler squeezing the life out of them. Henry and CF alternated the ironing, and when the last clothes were being finished, the rain slowed to a gentle shower.

We all gathered by the fire until Jacque had a stew ready for supper. It finally stopped raining as we were eating our meal. The entire day was bleak, wet, and uncomfortable. The gold in our pouches did nothing to lighten our gloomy moods.

We had hardly finished supper when Daan woke up and began crying uncontrollably. When he got more in control of himself, I asked,

"How are you now, Daan? It felt like we would never free you. Sorry, it took time to get you unpinned from under the flume."

"I'm not sure what I did before hooking up with you fellows, but you have helped me when I was in a couple of real fixes. I thank you. I panicked, believing you would leave me pinned and take my gold and be gone. I thought I would die alone, trapped in my greed for gold. I am ashamed of myself for thinking you would take advantage of my accident."

We might have talked further, but two men arrived from one of the other mining groups on Emory. They needed help. They reported that the rain had caused a mudslide at their operation, and one of them had broken his leg. The injured man had hobbled to our camp with his arm around his friend's neck and a stick crutch to keep the weight off his damaged limb. The leg was severely bruised along the shin and the skin was scraped. He said it was excruciatingly painful, and I saw that it looked swollen. Upon my examination, I could thankfully report that his leg was not broken. The man was relieved, but he had exhausted himself thinking about how he would manage with a broken leg. I cleansed and wrapped the leg and invited the man to rest in the shack, along with Dutch Dan, overnight.

Jacque, Mean Mike, and CF went to their tents to sleep, and Henry and I stayed in the shack and kept a small fire and a steady watch over both wounded men. Henry slept first, awakening partway through the night to relieve me so I could rest a little also. Instead of me getting any sleep, though, I stayed up the rest of the night talking with Henry.

"It seems like this sluicing work with Dutch Dan and the mud are troubling you, Henry," I said to him.

"Nothing, in the time you have known me, have I ever mentioned my father to you?" Henry asked me.

"Not as I recall, but you have talked of being the third son in an old English family which is in financial trouble," I answered him.

"That was my story to tell until recently. You may remember that I received an important letter at Yale, from a lawyer in London, England. It brought me word that my father recently died due to a riding accident in a fox hunting event."

I looked at Henry in surprise and sadness, and I whispered, "I'm sorry, Henry."

Henry simply continued with his anguished words. "My oldest brother died of a childhood disease and until his death, he had been in line to acquire Father's estates and hereditary titles. So than, Stanley, my second older brother, was set to inherit them. While waiting to obtain his estates and titles, Stanley successfully partnered with a wealthy middle-class businessman. He became a part-owner in a factory. Stanley was the pride of my father, while I was the insignificant third son. I was seen as destined for a simple position in the army or church. I asked to be allowed to go to one of England's colonies, preferably Upper Canada, for a year or two before settling into one of the positions awaiting me, which my father would decide," Henry explained, pausing because Dutch Daan was muttering in his sleep.

"So, you came to this new British colony with your father's blessing," I asked Henry.

"Not really," he continued, "I had serious issues with my father and brother. They prided themselves as the privileged upper class, while only tolerating the wealthy middle class and ignoring the working class. As a member of parliament, my father voted against the Factory Act of 1832, which stopped children under the age of nine working in factories and mines for long hours and little pay. My father and brother had no concern for the terrible slums of the laborers and poor or their lack of education and health services." Henry stopped when Mean Mike and King wandered into the shack to see if we were okay.

"I guess King could hear your voices, and he was restless and had to see what was going on," Mike explained. King had marched in and sat at Henry's feet, as if he needed to hear what Henry was saying.

Henry said, "I have been trying to tell Nothing that Dutch Daan frustrates me like my father did. My father was always quick to bark orders, and he refused to consider anything that contradicted his ideas, and that is how I find Dutch Daan. He has to control every-thing and everyone instead of allowing us to use common sense and pay attention to rain and mud, and then work according to those conditions," Henry said in honest frustration, but he was startled and shaken when a voice cut in after he finished speaking.

"I agree with you," Dutch Daan said, sitting up from his sleep-ing position. "I hope you'll give me another chance to be better at working with you. I realize I drive workers away and ruin the success we might achieve. I have been listening to your words, and I realize you are an educated man and worthy of my respect." Then he added, "Sorry, but I have to lie down again," and he did and was asleep in seconds. I checked his forehead and noted that he was a bit warm.

"I am concerned that Dutch Daan is a bit feverish. I will check him with my thermometer in an hour or so to see if it is growing more serious. Henry, I think you may have more to share about your father."

Henry did not hesitate, as if he needed to get his tale uncov-ered before us. He continued, "My father did not want me to go to Upper Canada, as he had no connections there with the people in government. He allowed me to come to British Columbia because he could follow my progress here through the Colonial Office under his friend, Lord Lytton, who hand-picked Richard Moody to be the founder of this new colony. My father, with connections in the

Colonial Office, had a hand in the appointment of Chief Justice Matthew Begbie to this colony. My father's plan was that if I took part in the gold rush in this new wilderness territory, I would very soon appreciate my upper-class birth. My progress was to be reported to him when my readiness to return to England and assume a dignified life reflective of my heritage, was apparent to my father's connections here. If I dared to turn my back on my class, my father would have been socially embarrassed and personally mortified," Henry said in great sadness.

"Henry, you are avoiding telling us something. I can sense you're hiding something. Are you regretful that your father died from an accident while you were here in British Columbia?"

"I am shocked that my father was killed by a horse stumbling in a fox hunt. The horse went down with a broken leg, pinning him under its weight. I have always thought of my father as bigger than death, but that's only half my distress." Henry stopped, unable to speak for a few seconds, and he gasped out in genuine anguish, "My brother Stanley is dead also. I have been summoned home to take over my father's estates, wear his titles, and manage the sizable holdings of my dead brother's factory and his family. The very clutches of upper-class responsibility, duty, conformity, and domination of individuals has been thrust on my shoulders. It is like a noose about my neck that is threatening to strangle me."

After a pause to allow Henry a chance to collect himself, I asked, "Henry, how did your brother Stanley die?"

"As a result of a machinery accident at his factory. Apparently, Stanley was checking on a production problem with a foreman when a steam compressor exploded. Both men died in the mishap," Henry said bitterly, and then added, "Stanley has a wife and seven children to be provided for in a country manor house."

"How close to your father's death was Stanley's?" I asked in curiosity.

"Two days after Father's funeral," Henry snapped in anger.

We remained silent, and then Mean Mike said, "I resented the orders of my old man. You could not tell him anything either. I realize now he was doing what he felt was best for me. Maybe it was the same for your father. As I see it, he helped you to be a decent, honest person, who is needed in every class of people. For sure, you'll carry your family heritage with intelligence, fairness, good manners, and courage. Don't sweat it lad, you'll improve the English upper class. You need to return for your mother and other family members, as they need you to take charge and help them through the death of your father and brother."

"I know I do," said Henry, "But I have time for now, as nothing takes more time than London lawyers and the inheritance of wills and deeds of estates in England. I will be able to be with you for a few months yet."

"We will be sad to lose you Henry, but if you need to return home to your family sooner, we will understand," I told him.

"The lawyer's letter indicates the legal paperwork for the rights of succession will be ready on or before December 15, 1860. The legal descriptions of estates, properties, lands, and tallies of assets and liabilities will all be ready on that date for my signature. My inherited titles to be recognized as of December 15, 1860, forth-with," Henry explained.

I suggested that Henry needed to get some more sleep in our tent, and he left broken in spirit and grief. I looked at Mean Mike, who said when Henry was well out of hearing. "Ye know Nothing, I could handle the title of Duke or Earl. Why I'd not object to Lord Mike or Your Majesty! I likely will be a blacksmith and never be honored with anything more than being called, Smithy."

"I'll have to wait until heaven to be called anything but short. Not that it bothers me, more than having my eye pulled out of its socket. You can vouch that I have mastered all my anger and resentments and am kind and levelheaded at least 51 percent of the time," I joked.

"I can say in all honesty ye be like a stick of dynamite 49 percent of the time, but that is not as bad as your bossiness. You act like you are seven feet tall, giving orders right and left. Even King is afraid of you," Mike said with his stupid grin and a smirk.

"I can see you have no respect for me, but someday I may operate on ye, and ye will respect my shaking hand and spiteful memory on the operating table," I said, enjoying the banter with Mike.

Dutch Daan was very subdued the following morning, and his fever wasn't completely gone. He insisted on going with us to the mining site. He said that he was too sore to work but would be resting nearby if we had any questions. He surprised us by saying, "I trust you to run things while I am laid up. I can wash and sort the gold you find. I'm putting Mike in charge of the irrigation ditch, which I usually do. Henry and Jacque, I ask you to reset the flume and anchor it better than I did. Nothing, you are in charge of the rockers."

Dutch Daan observed our work and never criticized us, but he did offer suggestions very carefully. He treated us as if we knew as much as him. Our spirits soared, and Dutch Daan was in enough pain to be glad to let us have more freedom. He was amazed that we actually had more gold than usual collected at the end of the day.

By supper, Dutch Daan was running a high fever, and we brought over his tent from his camp and set it up, so I could check his shoulder and arm and watch him more closely. The scrapes on his arm and shoulder were slightly infected, and I cleansed and dressed them. I tried to lower Daan's fever with cool cloths. I insisted he try to get extra sleep, and he did not object.

The man with the injured leg who had stayed with us overnight had returned to his camp in the morning, but one of his partners came back in the evening to see if I would come and treat the man's leg once again. It wasn't far away, but Henry insisted on going with me. CF was at camp most of the day, so he wanted to come as well to have a chance to visit with us walking to the camp and back.

Henry walked with the man from the neighboring camp, and they led the way. CF and I followed, and he looked for berries and plants for food. CF was able to spot a game trail that would be important for future hunting. We walked quickly because we wanted to be back before dark. When we arrived at the camp, I went right to work cleansing the man's leg and dressing it. His leg also was infected, and I asked him to come to our camp tomorrow evening, and I would treat it again. If he was not able to come on his own, he was to send his friend again to get me. While I was treating his leg, the miners at his camp showed Henry and CF the destruction the mud slide had caused at their diggings. They were discouraged about getting things in working order again. We promised to ask Dutch Daan if he could come over and give them advice in starting over.

It was a deep dark as we walked back toward our camp, but CF was sure that he could see the path enough to get us back. Both Henry and I were confident we were in good hands. We did not talk, as CF was concentrating on the path to get us home. He stopped suddenly and put his finger in front of his lips. We could hear whispering coming from ahead of us. There was a flicker of light. We strained our ears and our eyes to determine who it was.

As we stretched our necks and heads, we surely heard a woman's voice. CF whispered, "Maggie Kelly," and Henry and I each whispered back, "I think so too."

Henry spoke loudly, "Excuse us, but is that you, Miss Kelly, ahead of us?"

"Yes, it's me, but who is it hiding in the dark there? I warn you; Constable Dunn is with me."

Before Henry could answer her, a young male voice said, "I am Constable Dunn, and we are looking for the camp of Mike Duncan."

I asked, "Would Mike Duncan be also called Mean Mike?"

"I'm not certain, but the man who signed at auction for buying the bluetick coonhound wrote his name as Mike Duncan," the voice ahead of us answered.

Henry answered back, "We are on the way to his camp, and we can take you there. I am Henry Arden, and Constable Dunn, you gave me a letter from Judge Begbie."

"I remember you, sir, and the other fellow with you that day. We would be glad of your assistance," Constable Dunn replied.

CF led us as a group to our camp with himself first, Maggie Kelly and the constable next, followed by Henry and me. It wasn't long until we were at the three-sided shack surprising Mean Mike, Jacque, and Dutch Daan.

The young constable wasted no time and was very professional in explaining that two men were going about Yale saying that the big guy Mike who bought the coonhound was the one who had shot the dog's owner in the back. The constable confirmed that there was a cut-throat bunch at Yale practicing vigilantism, who, he explained, were always trying to undermine the constables and British rule and authority. Many of them were crooks and criminals who loved to stir things up to harm individuals that they wanted to suffer or die. This self-appointed group had no legal authority but set themselves up to punish people for unproven accusations, and too often in the past, they had succeeded. The constable said that he had come to warn Mike that the group was waiting for him to show up in Yale with the dog so that they could lynch him.

The constable also explained why they came to our camp so late. He said that Maggie Kelly had come to him a couple of days ago, to report she had heard the rumors against Mike in her café. She wanted Mike warned, but he needed to check her story out, and when he did, he learned that Mike was in danger.

Maggie said she would help the constable reach Mike. She knew a little of Emory, as she had a food place at Hill's Bar when it was busy and bustling in its past. Maggie said that she could get the constable to Emory, and it shouldn't be hard to find Mike's camp. Tonight, she could not leave the café until after supper and upon reaching Emory, it was sunset. They had followed several trails without success and were almost ready to return to their canoe when we found them.

Dutch Daan informed Constable Dunn that it was Rod Murdock, Lemon Jim, and Frenchy and his brothers who were stirring up trouble for Mean Mike and all of us if they could.

Constable Dunn stated, "All of those you have mentioned are crooks and trouble-makers. We know they are all part of the criminal element at Yale. They tend to be there for a time, then be gone for a while, then come back again. We would love to jail them all, and we will eventually. The good news is that many of them will move on with the gold rush as it moves away from the Fraser Canyon. They are a nest of rattlesnakes that we have to deal with for now."

Mean Mike asked the constable, "So what do you want me to do? Should I stay out of Yale, or can I come, but not with the dog?"

"I think that it would be best to stay out of Yale for a good while because it's hard for the group to keep people stirred up against you if they don't see you," Dunn offered.

Dutch Daan asked, "I need to go to Yale often. Do I need to watch for this group, as they know that Mean Mike and his partners work with me? They might have even followed you here."

"Do you think they are after all of you and hoping to put you on the run if they lynch Mean Mike?" Dunn asked Dutch Daan.

"With those villains, I'd say that's about the size of it," Daan replied.

"That being the case, I think it's time to spread some lies of our own. I propose we poke the snake's den. Are you fellows, and Miss

Kelly, ready to act like criminals yourselves?" Constable Dunn said mischievously. It was at dawn when CF and Mike escorted Maggie and the constable to their canoe. It had taken most of the night to lay out plans as to how we might skin a whole mess of rattlers.

CHAPTER THIRTEEN:
Handling the Snakes Very Carefully

SKINNING A WHOLE den of rattlers was not about spreading falsities to nudge the snakes out into the open. Not every suggestion is a good one. When the constable suggested we spread lies and act like criminals ourselves, I surprised the constable with a firm, "No, sir. I agree people love to hear lies, but the power over them is the truth. I say that we fight lies with truth."

"I agree with you in principle, but I have found criminals like Rod Murdock, Lemon Jim, and the others pay more attention to lies than the truth. How would telling the truth turn out to be anything more than them denying the truth? Their word against ours?" the constable asked me, an impatient edge to his voice.

"A rattlesnake is much better at being a rattlesnake than I could ever be. Likewise, I believe the men stirring up trouble for Mike, Daan, and all of us will be much better than us at a lying. What will either make them run or strike out at us is the truth because they cannot change that. The truth stands that Rod Murdock killed Faro dealer Smith, and he had the dead body of his partner buried.

Murdock can deny these things, but he cannot change that truth. The more he hears that people are speaking the truth about him, he will either slither away or act out and get his head chopped off. The same goes for Lemon Jim," I said stubbornly.

"What truth do we have to tell about Lemon Jim and Rod Murdock?" the constable questioned skeptically.

"How about a Wanted poster on your office door and displayed a few places around Yale asking for the truth. It could read:

'Reward for Information Concerning:
The whereabouts of Lemon Jim,
owner of a bluetick coonhound.
Wanted in the investigation into the
mistaken identity of a dead body found
in Yale falsely identified as Lemon Jim.

Lemon Jim is alive.

Information resulting in the locating
of Lemon Jim for questioning will result
in a reward.

Details at the constable's office.'"

Dutch Daan spoke up quickly, "I would put up some reward money."

After silence and thought, Dunn thought that the chief constable would likely agree to such a poster.

"What truth could we spread about Rod Murdock?" Henry asked.

"Tell us, Nothing, since you want us to use truth to our advantage," Mean Mike prodded me.

"Well, we know Rod Murdock let Smith die instead of helping him when he was shot. Did Murdock kill his partner Max Piketon his partner, or just pick his pockets when he was dead? I would need Alf and Dino to go over the truth again. How do you fellows remember the events of Smith's shooting? I already questioned the others, and they admitted they needed Alf and Dino to make sure we had the clear truth about Murdock.

Jacque said, "I suggest another Wanted poster, which reads:

'Reward for Information:
Missing person Max Piketon
Last seen in partnership with Rod Murdock.
The following men may have information
regarding Max Piketon:
Bill Talon, Jeff Landers, Frank Cross,
Bow-legged Bill, AND Old Kelly

Reward for Information Concerning Max.
Details at Constable's'"

"How did ye remember all the men that were with Rod Murdock?" Mike asked Jacque in surprise.

"Some of them were once fur traders, one is Jeff Landers, the other Frank Cross. They never have been honest men. Bill Talon, Bow-legged Bill, and Old Kelly, I know from trading at Hudson Bay Company forts. Alf and Dino also said that they are men to look out for, as they are willing to lie and cheat, and they will be interested in a reward. I think Rod Murdock will be concerned with these men betraying him if they have a chance to get reward money," Jacque stated.

Henry responded, "The truth of the disappearance of his partner could well rattle Rod Murdock. The men with him when his partner went missing could also start squirming and rattling for the reward money"

I asked the constable, "Are the men mentioned in the two posters part of the vigilante group?"

"Often they are," he answered.

Maggie Kelly stated, "The posters will be a good start, but many men at Yale do not read or will not necessarily see them. The people named in the posters will be quick to tear them up when no one is about. I will display one on a wall inside my café, and they need to be placed in other spots like the Hudson Bay's Company post and the steamer office, to name a couple. I will spread the word of truth among those who dine at the café. Jacque, you need to talk to workers at the fort because they trust you. A poster there will be seen by many."

"I will make two posters right now, as soon as I get my straight pen, nibs, ink, and paper," Henry remarked, heading to his tent. He was back in no time.

We watched Henry make two official looking and clear posters. His steady hand and clear printing with pen and ink were impressive, and his use of a wide flat-point pen nib was skilled. When finished, Henry said, "It is a start for the constable's office door. I will make more and get them to Dunn in the days ahead, but this is a beginning."

CF asked, "Posters may stir the snakes to come out of their den, but will we hear them rattle before they strike at us? What lies constable have to help stir up the rattlers?

"The fabrication I considered was this: Mean Mike is supposedly injured in an accident at his mining site, cannot work, and is putting the coonhound up for auction at Dunn's office again. The chief constable would again oversee the auction at a particular day and time. This would pressure Lemon Jim to try and steal the dog before the auction or take the dog by force at the auction. Hopefully, we could catch him when he tried to seize King," the constable explained.

"Perhaps Lemon Jim would just get someone to bid on the dog for him," I objected.

"That is the weakness with that lie, but how does this one sound: Dutch Daan lets it be known that he has prospered well and is taking his foreman Mean Mike and his dog with him to Holland. Mean Mike and his dog are really going with him to protect him because he is carrying a large amount of gold. The date for their departure is disclosed. Once again, Lemon Jim, Rod Murdock, Frenchy, and his brothers will be after both Daan's gold and Mike's dog. We need to be ready for them," the young constable offered with some noticeable enthusiasm.

"The way I see it, the truth puts the focus on the criminals, while the lies make Mike, Daan, and all of you bait to be attacked by the men who are now just talking against you," Maggie Kelly spoke out. Then she added, as we were all listening to her, "I like the idea of the posters best, in fact, a weekly newspaper sheet would help encourage law and order and give reasons for the crooks to move on willingly. A weekly newspaper sheet of ten copies posted about Yale could focus on new gold strikes that are occurring beyond the Fraser in the interior. This news will increase the willingness of our crooks to move on. As a business owner, I would like to see a newspaper sheet to help build and promote Yale as a permanent community of safety, law, and order."

"Maggie's ideas are excellent. With the help of our group, I could manage a handmade weekly newspaper sheet of sorts. Maggie and the constable would need to feed us what is happening and being said at Yale. We could make a small news sheet slanted in truth and purpose for a permanent community at Yale, as a supply center for the gold rush," Henry said.

"Constable, do you see your boss being against the posters or a newspaper sheet?" I asked.

"I will gladly show them to him, and then I'll put them up on the outside of our office door if the chief has no objections. The newspaper sheet would not need his permission, but maybe a few words from him in it might be a good idea for everyone's benefit," the constable answered.

"I will complete three or four more posters plus the same number of newspaper sheets in a few days. That will give us time to see if your chief constable approves, and then he can see them first-hand," Henry said.

"By then I will hear if the wanted posters have sparked any discussion in the café crowd," Maggie said.

"I will be able to report if there are inquiries about the amount of each reward offered," the constable added. Then he asked, "Could someone guide Miss Kelly and me to the river to locate our canoe and head for Yale?"

Jacque and CF not only escorted them to their canoe but accompanied them in one of ours until they were well on their way to Yale. It was sunrise when CF and Jacque returned to camp.

The next week was busy with sluicing, and Henry enlisted us to help with the newspaper sheets. A natural artist, CF drew a Union Jack flag at the top of each, then if there was room at the bottom or side, he drew a realistic animal, bird, river, forest, or mountain scene. *Yale Bulletin* was followed by a number, the month, and year. We were pleased with our first edition that read:

(Top of sheet drawing of the Union Jack)

Yale Bulletin # 1 August 1860

Written at Yale, British Columbia
Yale is the Steamship terminus to the
Fraser River Canyon.
It is the doorway for finding gold
beyond the canyon and the interior.

Editor's Words:

The Yale Bulletin encourages the growth of a safe law-abiding community for miners passing through Yale on their search for gold, and for the merchants, business owners, and British government officials who call Yale home.

Together we can increase safety and reduce theft, drunkenness, assaults, and the crimes of those who take the law into their own hands.

The constable's office, with the assistance of Judge Matthew Begbie, are to administer the law. Please note and act, if possible, upon the Wanted Posters on the constable office door to help them in their duty.

Please contact Constable Dunn with news or advertisements for this weekly Publication. News of church or school endeavors, trades, and services are encouraged for the Bulletin.

In Your Service,
H. S. Arden, Editor, and assistants
Union Jack Drawing by CF

A small but beautiful drawing of an eagle completed the page.

The chief constable was supportive of both the posters and the newspaper sheets. The newspaper sheets made Yale sound like a place of law and order rather than an anything-you-please locale. The newspaper production, which we kept at five sheets for the first weeks, was a welcome diversion from our steady daily routine of sluicing. Maggie Kelly's Chinese cook became a frequent visitor, bringing information or feedback for the bulletins. Constable Dunn would watch for any of us coming to Yale to discuss if there was interest in the rewards or tips about the location of both Rod Murdock and Lemon Jim.

The third-week Constable Dunn arrived at our camp, with word that a man named Bill Talon said he would take him to the hideout of Murdock and Lemon. The constable wanted us to accompany him and identify Lemon Jim. Dunn could then question him as to how his dog was with the dead man's body. He would also ask Rod Murdock about the disappearance of Max Piketon, his former partner.

Constable Dunn said, "I suspect both men will have only empty answers, but I can advise them to not leave Yale until our investigations concerning the dead body and the missing Max Piketon are over. I have hope it will encourage them to leave Yale quickly."

We all agreed it was worth a try and that some of us would go with the constable, but the sluicing and irrigation ditch also needed attention. Dutch Daan had anger in his heart toward both men. Henry had been with Lemon Jim on a hunting trip. Jacque and CF could scout out traps the group might walk into. They were all eager to accompany the constable. I offered to stay and work with Mean Mike at the sluicing. Mike could cover the irrigation ditch and help me with the sluice box off and on. Th production would be less than normal, but it would have to work until the men got back from their trip with Constable Dunn.

Jacque, CF, Henry, Dutch Daan, and Constable Dunn set off to deal with Rod Murdock and Lemon Jim. As Mike, King, and me made our way to the irrigation ditch and our sluicing site, the dog was sniffing and whining quietly. Mike paused our trek to work and whispered to me, "There be people ahead waiting to discourage us and our gold operation or worse."

I grinned at Mean Mike, towering over me, and said, "Don't be afraid. King and me will leave you one or two to play with. Why don't you and King go up to the irrigation ditch and keep it from damage, and I will entertain those at our sluice box and rockers with my charm. In fact, I'm going into our work site, singing, praying, and preaching at the top of my lungs."

"Okay, Nothing," Mike whispered, "But I like you better when you behave like a doctor not a preacher. Come on, King," he said to the dog, and they disappeared through the woods up to Emory Creek and the irrigation dam.

I began singing loudly, a distorted version of Psalm 23.

"The Lord is my shepherd. I shall not want. I shall not want.

No gold for me. No gold for me. He makes me lie down in the mud.

No green pastures. No still waters. Only mud for me. Only mud for me.

I fear no evil. I fear no evil. He comforts me. He comforts me.

Glory to He, the shepherd of me. Glory be glory be,"

until I reached our work site.

As I entered into the openness of our sluicing site, I began a loud prayer, my eyes closed, "Lord, you are all wise and powerful, thank you that I can work with Mean Mike, who has the strength of Goliath, today. Bless the work of our hands this day and anoint us with your Spirit and overflow our cups with your love. Amen."

I opened my eyes to see three men staring at me. So, I said, like a man who blusters on never waiting for an answer, "Gentlemen, the revival meeting is not until this evening. But if it is sins you need to confess before then, I will hear you right away. Or if you need Holy Scripture for your encouragement, I will help you with that too. Now, if it is doctoring, you are needing from me, know that I cannot give a cure for the great pox called syphilis or the clap called gonorrhea." The three men looked at each other, stunned at my words.

One man spoke up in anger, "We did not come here for a preacher or doctoring. We're here to take over this sluicing operation."

"Well, you fellows look capable. Sure glad, you know what you are doing because we've had other fellows hire on and quit, mighty quick. It only takes the loss of a hand or arm to have people give up before they have been here a week or two," I told them.

The spokesman for the group said in impatient frustration, "Listen runt! We are taking over this mining site!"

"So, you said before. I'm not deaf. I am not preventing you from taking over the site. Dutch Daan was talking about selling the whole operation, so it must have happened. Is there something you need from me? Don't you know how to take over the site?" I asked him

"You can get the hell out of here, and don't come back!" the man yelled at me.

"Certainly sir. I'll leave right away. And to prove there are no hard feelings, I'll just pray for your new mining endeavor." And I began, "Dear Lord . . ."

"Stop it," he bellowed, "Just get out of here, damn you!" The two men with him were holding him back from coming after me.

"What is all the shouting about, Nothing?" Mike asked as he lumbered into the clearing with King.

"Mike, these fellows are taking over the ownership of this mining site. I'm sure they will enjoy it, but the guy they are holding is kinda high strung," I said.

Mike answered me, "Be kind lad. He probably cannot help himself. Maybe he was born bum first, as they say it makes a grown man always upset and not knowing what he should do."

"You are right! Some folks just get all riled up and have to be hung on to, as they're like a child with a bad temper and could hurt themselves," I said to Mike.

The two men holding onto their spokesman were unable to hold him any longer, and he broke free of them and ran at me, shouting, "I'll show you, runt, that I'm more than high strung, you jackass!"

Mike said to King, "Stop him." King let out a loud growl, showed his teeth, and sat alert, ready to attack the man if he continued to run toward me.

The man had excellent reflexes, for his rush toward me stopped as fast as it began. Standing with his pistol drawn, Mike said, "Give my partner your weapons, and prepare to confess your sins. Did Rod Murdock or Lemon Jim send you? I have an itchy finger and mean heart."

One of the men said, "Yes."

"I want you to meet two friends of yours who told me they were taking over the irrigation ditch. They are tied to trees until the constable comes, and you will now join them. They're near here. Nothing, bring some more rope for these visitors. We'll let them hug trees as they relearn the commandment, 'Don't steal.'" Mike stated.

I grabbed the rope, and with Mike and his pointed gun, as well as King to ensure obedience, we got the three men tied to trees near the other two, who were already pondering their bad conduct. We left the five men to their captivity.

Mike and I set about our daily work of sluicing with our limited manpower, and we had hardly begun when two fair-sized nuggets materialized in the sluice box. I had been shoveling the dirt into the container from a small but long ridge, so I continued to feed the sluice box with dirt from that ridge only. It was a dandy source of nuggets, which made our hearts skip a beat or two. Mike and I were intent on sluicing and were surprised to realize the sun was ready to set. We were becoming anxious that our partners and the constable had not returned from tracking down Lemon Jim and Rod Murdock.

Just as we were about ready to move our captives back to our camp, Constable Dunn, CF, Jacque, Dutch Daan, and Henry returned with prisoners of their own. They did not have Lemon Jim or Rod Murdock with them but Bill Talon, Frenchy, and his two brothers.

Constable Dunn wanted all the prisoners taken to jail at Yale first thing. We had five prisoners and they had four, so there were nine of them to transport. That meant three bound prisoners in three canoes: Jacque and Constable Dunn had Frenchy and his brothers, CF and Dutch Daan had Bill Talon and two of our prisoners, and Mean Mike and me took the other three men. It was dark when we finally got all the prisoners locked up at Yale. Mean Mike insisted we stop at Kelly's Café even though it was already closed.

We were not sure what Maggie Kelly would tell us. She might say that we were welcome, or she might say closed meant closed. After forceful knocking by Mike, the café door opened a crack, and a yawning voice said, "Who is it, and what do you want?"

Mike announced, "It's Mike. Your handsome fellow with his servants."

"Did you come to wash dishes and peel potatoes? I have no time for someone who thinks he's a handsome man and wants to be admired and waited on. If you have come to eat, I'll open the door," replied Maggie Kelly from behind the crack in the door.

"To be near your beauty lass and have some food, I'll wash dishes, peel potatoes, and be a slave to you!" Mike said with more than a little sincerity missing in his voice.

"Stop your blarney, Mike. It's late, and I'm tired. You can come in, but leave your guff at the door," Maggie stated firmly.

So, in we went, and Maggie was warm and friendly to us and a tad frosty to Mike. We crowded around one of the biggest tables in her café and waited as she put the kettle on for tea and looked in the kitchen for food. She told Mike he could help in the kitchen, and he went to help her like a dutiful child. We were all tired and glad to sit and relax. There was a confident silence between us that eventually we would hear about the capture of the prisoners in which we had not been involved.

In short order, we could hear the kettle whistling in the kitchen and a pan or two rattled. Maggie came to the table with two big loaves of beautiful baked bread on a cutting board and a container of butter. She asked Henry to come to the kitchen and bring out two pots of tea and cups for all, which he did.

Maggie returned with seven plates, which she asked me to set out, one for each of us and herself. She handed CF a bread knife and asked him to slice the two loaves. She put knives and forks in front of Jacque and asked him to pass them out, so everyone had one of each.

Minutes later, she hailed Dutch Dann to come to the kitchen to help carry out food. Dutch Daan returned from the kitchen carrying a platter of scrambled eggs in each hand. He was followed by Mean Mike, who had two platters of fried ham drizzled with honey.

Lastly, Maggie Kelly came from the kitchen carrying two platters of fried potatoes. When the food was placed on the table, Maggie

Kelly said, "Mike did the cooking, so if you have any complaints, they go to him. He has potential for becoming a decent cook. But if he ever wants a wife, he better get done looking for gold and stop chasing women."

Henry said both loudly and dead seriously, "If Mike doesn't want you for a wife, I do!" It turned silent and still with everyone feeling uncomfortable and wondering what Mean Mike would say or do.

I surprised myself by proclaiming. "Me too! I want Maggie for my wife, and I'm the only one here who knows how to truly relate to a short person."

The table broke into laughter, and CF said, "Miss Maggie want handsome, young man like me. Mike, Henry, and Nothing all too old."

"Stop it! Enough talk of husbands for me, as it is killing my appetite. Pass the food before it gets cold," Maggie commanded us. Which we did, and we enjoyed every mouthful of Mike's cooking.

CHAPTER FOURTEEN:
Decisions Greater Than Storing Up Gold

BEFORE WE LEFT Maggie's café, there was a knock at the door and Constable Dunn entered, reporting he had a message for me. It was word that Dr. John Sebastian Helmcken was to be in Yale the next two days, and he was open to meeting with me at the Hudson's Bay Company fort. The group, except for Henry, did not know that he might allow me to be his assistant and train under him, doctoring in Victoria.

When Dutch Daan heard I was to meet a Dr. John, he asked, "Is that the Dr. John in Victoria?" He knew the great reputation the physician had, and it was Dr. John who helped his partner know he had been slowly poisoned by Rod Murdock and Lemon Jim. "Have you worked with Dr. John before?" Daan asked me, determined it seemed to find out what my meeting with him was about. Thankfully, Maggie interrupted Dutch Daan, inviting Constable Dunn to have a cup of tea with us.

Constable Dunn poured himself a cup. He had hardly seated himself with us at the table when CF said, "Mike think Miss Maggie his girlfriend, but Henry, Nothing, and me want Maggie as wife. You want Maggie as wife?" Constable Dunn gasped, turned red, and said without hesitation, "Absolutely."

Once again, I broke an uneasy silence with, "He's too tall. Maggie will be happiest if she marries a short man just my size."

Maggie said in a strained tone, "If I hear one more word about me being somebody's wife, I will scream. You think being married is every woman's dream come true. For some, it is more like a night-mare. I buried my last husband, counting my blessings. If I ever want one of you as a husband, you will know it. I'll be the one asking a man to marry me, and he better be smart enough to say yes, or he will wish he hadn't hesitated." Then Maggie forced a smile and said, "Constable Dunn, please tell us what happened when you went to capture Rod Murdock and Lemon Jim."

He explained how Bill Talon had led them on their chase. In his gruff voice, he began, "Talon was sent to bring us into an ambush spot by Frenchy and his two brothers. We figured this would be the case, so CF and Jacque had separated from us as we went along, scouting ahead for a likely trap or ambush spot. As we came closer, Bill Talon lost his nerve, and he warned Daan, Jacque, and me that Frenchy and his brothers were waiting to kill us on orders of Murdock and Lemon. Talon wanted no part of the murders. He wasn't sure if Frenchy and his brothers might not have orders to kill him too. We appreciated him alerting us and followed him with our guns, ready to fire. But arriving at the ambush location, we saw that CF and Jacque had already taken care of Frenchy and his brothers, who had been drinking. They were not as alert as they might have been if they had been sober. Jacque or CF, tell them what you did," the constable said, looking from one to the other.

CF said, "When I climbed a tree to see enemy. Tree had bees' nest branch above. I saw Frenchy and his brothers below. They waiting to attack as Talon led the others closer. I made a bird call to my father, who answered with another bird call. Frenchy and his brothers paid no attention to our signals and did not even look up for any birds near them. I could reach the bees' nest and hit it with the back of my bow. It fell near the men below, and angry bees swarmed out. Frenchy and his brothers were watching the bees swarming near them. Father easily came up beside them and told them to drop their guns. I helped guard them. We warned Talon and the others to come to us and to stay away from angry bees. The constable arrested Frenchy and his brothers."

"Once again, CF frustrated Frenchy and his brothers, and he has earned their deepest and purest hatred," Dutch Daan commented.

"Frenchy and his brothers will not say where Murdock and Lemon are at, but I have a feeling that they think they will rescue them," offered Constable Dunn.

"Is your office escape proof?" Henry asked.

"It has been so far, but gunpowder could blow a hole in the logs. Nothing is escape proof when people are both stupid and desperate," the constable said in a very tired voice. He then thanked Maggie for the tea and bid us good night.

Mike said we had to get the dishes done and get out of the café, as Maggie had an early morning. To that, Maggie agreed, but six in the kitchen was too many, so Mike, CF, and me stayed to clean up, and the other three left. We had the dishes washed and dried and put away in quick order under Maggie's firm direction. As she ushered us out the door so she could lock it, she gave each of us a sincere thank you. None of us were sure what to make of Maggie when it came to marriage, but I thought that we were all ready to say yes without delay if she ever asked any of us.

The next day was an anxious one for me, as I had asked the constable to inform Dr. John that I would meet with him early in the evening. All day, I was preoccupied with thoughts of being a student of such an experienced and highly qualified doctor. Would he be a patient teacher? What would he want of me as his assistant? Would he expect me be his servant rather than a trusted colleague? Did he actually want an assistant? Would he help me train as a qualified and licensed doctor? Would he want me to become a valued partner to him through the years ahead in this colony?

I met Dr. John at the fort, and he informed me that I was highly recommended to him by Dr. Smith of the Royal Engineers. His first question to me was why I would want to be his assistant.

I explained that I hoped to become fully trained in medicine, doctoring, and surgery. I understood that he, Dr. John, sometimes had an assistant. I hoped that I might learn from him to be able to take medical examinations in England to be a licensed physician in the future. Honestly and frankly, I said, "I want to learn from you and doctor alongside you. Is this something you want?"

Dr. John replied, "As a young man, for two years, I was a runner delivering medicine to patients of Doctor Graves. He was the good doctor who agreed I could be his apprentice as a chemist and druggist. I understand about learning by doing and completing studies gradually. I have two passions: one of course is doctoring, and the other is politics. I have been the speaker of the legislative assembly on Vancouver Island since 1856, and I am married with a family, so an assistant can be extremely useful to me. Someone who wants to one day be fully licensed is preferrable, and it would mean living in Victoria, as I do. I may sometimes send my assistant to Hudson's Bay Company forts along the coast on Vancouver Island, as well as here in British Columbia if I am pleased their doctoring. How does all of this sound to you?"

I said, "It sounds excellent. How soon would you want me as an assistant, as I have given my word to work in a sluicing project near here for a period of time, and it may end quickly or go on for a month or two?"

Dr. John replied, "I could use the time until you are finished your work here to prepare for your arrival. I will contact Dr. Smith and find out the things you are competent at in general doctoring. I understand you doctored the sappers, and I could use you at the jail. As a chemist and druggist, I have many medicines that I will want you to be familiar with for treatments. I need to consider how to train you best in the use of the medical supplies that I have." Dr. John continued, "One last thing. Your salary will depend on how much responsibility I can entrust you with. When I was an apprentice, it was low at first but grew over time with experience and responsibility. Please give me your answer right away. Will you be my assistant?"

My mouth fell open in surprise at Dr. John's demand for a decision so quickly. My mind locked into what I had been hoping would happen at this meeting. I had already said yes in my mind and heart, and now I had the opportunity make my hopes come true. I paused, slightly took a deep breath, and then said, "Yes, I will be your assistant, as soon as my work here is complete."

Dr. John stood, outstretched his hand, and said, "We will shake on it to make it official," which we did. He then said to me, "I am pleased with your swift reply. Good doctors need to make quick decisions, as patients can die if are they are indecisive and unwilling act fast."

"Glad I passed the first test," I said.

"So am I," Dr. John exclaimed. "I will see you in Victoria when you get there. Good evening." And with that, he left me, stunned and amazed. I managed a quick, "Good night," in reply as he disappeared from the room.

In time, I would learn Dr. John was an abrupt person who discussed what was needed and nothing more. Having an assistant didn't mean he wanted to be friends with me. It would be, in his words, a professional relationship for our mutual benefit.

CF and Henry had insisted on coming with me, and they were waiting outside the fort. I suggested we go to the café for some celebratory dessert and coffee, to which they agreed.

When we arrived at Maggie's, Jacque, Mean Mike, and Dutch Daan were waiting for us. Maggie had no pie left, so we all enjoyed a slice of cake and a coffee before I shared about my meeting.

Maggie was able to join us, and she had heard of Dr. John as being a head doctor with the Hudson's Bay Company.

When the cake plates were all empty, Henry said, "Nothing, we have waited long enough. Out with it. Are you going to be an assistant to Dr. John?"

They looked at me, waiting for an answer, and I found myself choked up and managed a gasping, "Yes."

"When will this happen?" Dutch Daan asked in alarm.

"When I complete sluicing with you," I replied.

"Will you be living in Victoria?" Mike inquired.

"Mostly, but I could also be sent to help at any Hudson's Bay Company fort," I answered.

Maggie looked at me, and I felt that she was actually interested and concerned about me as she asked, "Is this what you hoped would happen, Nothing?"

"Yes, it's a great opportunity to learn from such a skilled doctor."

"I am glad for you," Maggie said, and she gave me a quick hug that melted my heart and rattled my brain. It was an enjoyable time together in the café with the presence of Maggie, and none of us were eager to head back to camp. We were the only customers in the eatery.

Our comfortableness was shattered when Lemon Jim and Rod Murdock came through the door with guns in their hands. They advanced quickly to our table, and we were taken off guard. We acted like statues as they marched up to us, bold as skunks ready to spray.

"Don't anyone move unless you want to die! We came for Dutch Daan and his gold. We will take what he has and what you mud grubbers have on you as well. Then we will take the Dutchman to his camp for his gold there, and we will also check your camp," Rod Murdock stated with authority, his gun pointing at us.

"Wait a minute!" I shouted, "I know you are a thief and a killer, but even a hopeless wretch like you needs to be warned so he can repent before his death. Do you two understand that your lives are in great danger at this very moment?"

"Shut up, runt," Murdock snarled. "We're holding guns on you bunch of maggots! Are you blind as well as stupid? We're not in danger you dumb ass! You might be the first I shoot."

"Don't shoot. I'm standing up, as I cannot sit and watch you be gunned down when I could prevent it." I stood up and both Lemon Jim and Rod Murdock looked at me like I was loco.

"Do you want to shoot him?" Murdock asked his partner. Before Lemon Jim could answer, I shouted, "As surely as I stand before you, your blood will be on your own hands! You two are headed for hell. Listen to me before it is too late!"

"I heard you was a crazy and self-made preacher, but we have no time for a lunatic like you. Just shut up, or I 'll shoot you right in that yapping trap of yours," Lemon Jim bellowed.

"Wait, you two fools! I want to spare your lives. Get out of here now. The café's cook has a shotgun pointed at you." I turned toward the kitchen and called out, "Have mercy on them, Wong Lee!"

With their guns in their hands, Murdock and Lemon quickly looked toward the kitchen door. All eyes were on Wong Lee, slightly peering out. Both men took quick shots at him, then turned and ran for the front door, not wanting to catch a blast from the kitchen doorway.

Lee opened the kitchen door and bowed slightly when Lemon and Murdock were gone. He lifted his hand, which held a pot! There was no shotgun in the kitchen because Maggie carried a small pistol in her apron pocket.

We knew it was not the end of Murdock and Lemon Jim, but it proved they were still around spying on Dutch Daan and his search for gold. It was certain Lemon Jim had not forgotten about King either. Maggie was really upset that Wong Lee could have been hit by a bullet and that I endangered his life. She was so angry that she told all of us to get out of her café. I was sorry to have Maggie angry at me, and I felt guilty that my bluffing could have hurt or killed Wong Lee. I avoided the café for a couple of weeks to allow Maggie to forgive me, and I hoped one day she would allow me to come back.

The sluicing remained profitable as the days played out in our agreement with Dutch Daan. We had said that after a month, we would discuss continuing if we were finding a good amount of gold. We could not deny our sluicing was doing well and felt obliged to do another thirty days with him. The second month was uneventful at the mining site, and the production of the weekly *YALE BULLETIN* gave us a steady extra project.

Partway through the second month, Constable Dunn came to our camp to discuss a situation with us. A U.S. marshal on a fugitive hunt had stopped at the constable's office to introduce himself and to inform law officials in Yale that he was searching for a woman in connection with a murder five years ago in Montana.

He was personally involved in the case, as the woman had murdered her husband—his brother. The marshal had the attitude of a bounty hunter to Constable Dunn, and he was alarmed when the marshal described the woman as young, tiny in build, pretty, and who spoke with a Scottish accent. Her name before marriage was Colleen Campbell. The constable said he thought there was a lady of pleasure at Hope with the name Colleen, so the marshal went to check it out.

Mean Mike spoke up, "I was a bit startled when Maggie said, 'I buried my last husband counting my blessings that he was dead and buried.'"

"That does not mean she killed him. He might have died of natural causes. Not all husbands are lovable," I said.

"Not all wives are lovable either," Jacque said from personal experience.

"The point is, I think we must all try to get Maggie to marry one of us, so we can protect her from the marshal," Constable Dunn blurted out.

CF spoke first, "I want Maggie as wife but not now—I too young now."

Jacque said, "I already have three wives. No more for me at this time anyway."

Dutch Daan stammered, "I'm too old and sort of already have a wife in Holland, except she is now married to my old partner."

The constable said to Mike, "You must have thought about marrying Maggie already?"

Mean Mike said, "Yes and no. Yes, she's pretty and charming, but Maggie isn't fooled by my flirting. She knows I'm not ready for a wife any time soon. Maggie is too wise to tolerate a trifler like me."

What about you, Constable? I remember at the café, you said that you would absolutely marry Maggie," I questioned.

Constable Dunn blushed a bright red as he had at the café, and he sputtered out, "I did say that, but I'm a confirmed bachelor till the day I die."

"I wouldn't be surprised if I remain a bachelor, as I'm short and ordinary. I would be thrilled to have Maggie as my wife, but she is pretty and could have the pick of any number of handsome suitors. I will do my best to get Maggie to ask me to marry her but if she does, it will be a divine miracle," I announced.

Henry spoke up then and said, "Maggie Kelly is the prettiest woman I have ever seen. She's smart, she makes people welcomed and honored in her café, and she is capable and very gracious at the same time. I can think of no one who would make my returning to England and upper-class suffocation more bearable. If she went with me to England, she would be safe from marshals and bounty hunters. I too will do my best to get Maggie to propose to me," Henry passionately proclaimed.

"We can only hope Maggie can decide on one of you two. I will alert you when the marshal returns from Hope," Constable Dunn confirmed, then left our camp.

Mike, CF, Jacque, and Dutch Daan all had their opinions on who Maggie might propose to between Henry and me. CF said that Maggie would not want either of us, as he was sure we were both too old.

Mike and Dutch Daan were certain that it wouldn't be me, as doctors are tied to their work and their wives and families suffer from neglect. Jacque said that Maggie would pick me for my kind heart and good understanding of others.

Henry and I met to discuss how we could best get Maggie to consider either of us for marriage. We knew Maggie always carried a small pistol in her apron pocket. Since it was questionable if she had murdered her previous husband, neither of us wanted to find out firsthand if Maggie was a killer.

I said to Henry, "Maggie seems so sweet and gracious, I don't think she would kill her husband except by an accident or if he was beating her."

"Those are my thoughts too," Henry agreed, also saying, "I think total honesty is best. We need to alert her to the visit of the marshal, and then Constable Dunn should tell Maggie what he told us. Next, we should tell Maggie we would like her to consider marrying one of us because either one of us would be thrilled to marry her. As a wife to you or I, we could discourage any discussion that she could be the woman the marshal is looking for in connection with the murder of his brother."

"Are you okay if Maggie admits to murdering her first husband?" I asked Henry.

"Yes, because it must have been an accident, or it was the only thing possible left for her to do," Henry said without hesitation.

"I'm hoping it is a case of mistaken identity and Maggie never killed anyone. Have you considered Maggie might see murder as her right since divorce is pretty rare for wife to obtain?" I asked Henry.

"I try not to think that is how Maggie deals with husbands, but we both know some men treat wives like a personal possession. I have wondered how some husbands live to an old age by the vile way they treat their wives and families," Henry answered.

"In fairness to husbands, some wives would seem to be ill-tempered and set on killing their husbands with criticism and fault-finding," I stated.

"One can only hope marriage can bring the best out in both husband and wife and their marriage is rich and full of love," Henry commented.

"Well said," I acknowledged. We decided we would try to talk with Maggie the next evening. We would not be forgetting the pistol in her apron pocket.

Events took a turn, however, and Henry and I did not get to talk with Maggie as planned. It was one of those days that happens around you and you just pick your way through broken glass. We had reached about midmorning sluicing when Wong Lee came with a message that I was needed to doctor Constable Dunn, who had been injured by an explosion at the jail—gun powder was used to blow a hole in the wall. It appeared that someone wanted Frenchy and his brothers out of jail and had been partly successful. The explosion had killed the person who set it off, none other than Rod Murdock. A chunk of log had hit him in his chest and came to rest protruding out his back. Inside the jail, one of Frenchy's brothers and Constable Dunn were badly hurt. Unfortunately, Frenchy and his other brother had escaped with the aid of a big man, likely Lemon Jim.

Dutch Daan allowed me, with the help of Henry, to go and doctor the constable and Frenchy's brother. By the time we reached the damaged office and jail, Frenchy's brother was dead. Other constables had cleared a good portion of the debris from the explosion and boarded up the hole in the wall caused by the explosion. Thankfully, the office was made of huge logs that had not shifted dangerously but tilted slightly toward its side, blasted open with gun powder.

Constable Dunn was stretched out on a cot, covered with a blanket, and he had a bandage on his head to stop the bleeding of his wound. He had been standing beside the desk when the explosion occurred, and the force of it had sent him flying headfirst into the nearest log wall. Other constables had found him crumpled beside the wall. Maggie Kelly had rushed to the jail and insisted the others not try to revive him or move him too much. They laid him on a cot, and as the doctor in Yale could not be found, she sent Wong Lee for me.

My examination found no lumps on his head, and the only wound I could find was a nasty scrape of skin off his forehead, which Maggie had carefully cleaned and bandaged well. I could not see signs of concussion but wanted to observe him for a little while, as his breathing was steady and his pulse just slightly elevated. He had no fever nor was he cool to the touch. As I was putting my thermometer away, Constable Dunn opened his eyes and said, "Nothing, why do I have ringing in my ears?"

"You lived through an explosion to the jail and bounced off a wall by its force. You, my friend, were beaten up by a blast of gun powder and are alive to rest and get your strength back."

"Why is my forehead so sore?' he questioned me.

"You scraped your skin on the wall when you were thrown about in the explosion. Give it a day or two, and you will be back to as good as new."

"Right now, I feel as weak as a new baby," Constable Dunn muttered and drifted off to a troubled sleep.

"Will he be, okay?" the chief constable asked me.

"I hope so. There doesn't seem to be serious outward injuries, but there could be internal ones that I cannot see right now. I will stay with him for a while to check on him. Is there anyone else that needs doctoring?" I asked.

"Actually, yes, there are three others who asked for our doctor. He was summoned to help an injured miner two days ago and has not returned. I'll take you to them," replied the chief constable.

It took about an hour and a half to take care of the three patients and when we returned, the constable was feeling much stronger, with little to no ringing in his ears. He was in no shape to return to work but able sit up on the cot and rest while regaining his strength.

Maggie Kelly burst into the office with a bowl of broth and hot from the oven biscuits for the ailing constable. It seemed like the perfect time to ask Dunn to tell Maggie about the visit of the marshal looking for someone he described as being herself. Henry and I were both there too, so we decided to deal with our plan to let Maggie know we each wanted to marry her.

The constable thanked Maggie for cleaning and dressing his head wound earlier. He also thanked her for the broth. At our urging, he alerted Maggie to the visit from Marshal Henry Plummer from Montana, who was searching for a woman who killed her husband—his brother—five years ago. The description of the woman seemed to fit Maggie. Although Dunn had not directed the marshal to her, he would likely come back in the days ahead. The constable asked Maggie directly, "Did you murder your husband five years ago?"

"Henry Plummer calls it murder, I call it self-defense," Maggie said evenly. "Does Plummer have any jurisdiction here in British Columbia?" Maggie asked the chief constable, who was also present.

"Not any legal authority, but often lawmen will be allowed to take an accused person back to face trial in their area, especially if the accused has been a troublemaker or criminal here. If the accused person has good standing in the community, a spouse or family, then often the officer is denied the authority to take them. That doesn't mean marshals and American bounty hunters haven't kidnapped the so-called accused and taken them illegally," the chief constable explained.

"Well, would you allow Henry Plummer to take me back to Montana for trial?" Maggie asked.

"I can deny Marshal Plummer, he can take my denial to court, and then Judge Begbie would decide your fate. The judge loves to eat but more so drink. If he eats at your café and has drinks there, he will not be in a hurry to let you go with the marshal. I have seen men like Plummer bring a lot of damaging evidence against the person they are after. Their position and evidence can sway a judge," the chief constable said, being as honest as possible with Maggie.

"Thank you, Constable Dunn and Chief Constable Bayford, for alerting me to the arrival of Marshal Plummer here at Yale. I need to get back to the café," Maggie said.

"Nothing and I will walk you there because we cannot go back to our mining without food," Henry was quick to say.

"You go ahead with Maggie, Henry," I said. "I will just check the constable's pulse and temperature one more time to make sure he is okay," I explained.

When Maggi and Henry had left, Constable Dunn said, "Nothing, you are you letting Henry get the chance to ask Maggie to marry him first. Do you have cold feet about having Maggie as your wife?"

"Not in the least. I think that Maggie is too pretty to be satisfied with the likes of me. Let handsome Henry, a fine gentleman with a title of heritage to offer, steal her heart. Maggie would also be safer in England than in Victoria. Henry is a good friend, and I would be genuinely happy for them Maggie chooses him. Knowing Maggie, though, I suspect she will not marry either of us unless she can see love developing and lasting for a lifetime between herself and one of us," I answered. In checking the constable, his pulse and temperature were good. The broth and biscuits made him feel much better, and he was walking about without dizziness. He was going to be fine.

When I got to the café, Henry was seated at a table, and I joined him there.

"We are having today's dinner special, which is beef stew with bread and butter," Henry announced.

"Did you have a chance to talk to Maggie about marrying her?" I asked Henry.

"Yes, he did," Maggie said, as she put two bowls of beef stew and a plate of bread and butter before us. "What do you know about England, Nothing?" she asked me.

"Not much, but I have found Henry, who is from there, to be a loyal and honorable friend. He is clever, well mannered, and able to work at anything. If I were you, I would definitely marry him and travel to England and have tea with the queen."

Maggie looked at Henry and asked, "Does your family really meet with the queen?"

"Mostly we are expected to attend certain events where she will be present. Rest assured we will not have tea with her majesty very often, but life as part of the upper class means endless events and social obligations," Henry said as if it was no more important than having a drink of water.

Maggie looked strangely unimpressed and left so there could be no more discussion with her about anything.

We joyfully ate the delicious meal. Everything was cleaned up quickly with our hearty appetites. Henry said to me, "I will let you pay Maggie," as he handed me his share of the cost of the meal. "I'll go wait at the canoe for you."

When I paid Maggie a few minutes later, I stammered and turned, red faced, and blurted out, "Maggie, you are a very fine woman. I see that you are very smart and capable. I hope to one day become a fully trained doctor, and I will always be studying and learning so I can help and heal people. A doctor's life is not his own, but I would do my honest best to share my life with you. If you asked me to marry you, I would love you as best I know how, but you could teach me how to love you better if I wasn't so good at it."

"Thank you, Nothing. I am honored that you would want me as your wife. I know you and Henry are trying to protect me and keep me from the marshal. I am touched by your offers. I will cherish them always."

I said to her, "I haven't had much practice at courting a lady. Please be patient with me."

"Your kindness and desire to protect me are more important than any courting you could do." She left for the kitchen, and I left in a daze for the canoe.

CHAPTER FIFTEEN:
Endings on Our Terms

TEN DAYS LATER, I said to Henry, "Our sluicing has seemed like four months instead of only two. The steady output of gold may keep us here like rich captives," I said, this as we knew Dutch Daan was eager for us to continue into a third month of partnership with him.

"I could do one more month, but then I must depart for England to arrive before December fifteenth and be ready to become a fully invested upper class bloke with more responsibility than I want," Henry mused.

"Are you feeling better about stepping into your father's and brother's shoes, Henry?" I inquired.

"Yes, I am more resigned to do my duty because my family needs me, but also know, that Maggie Kelly seems no more eager to ask me to be her husband than when I told her that I wished she would. Do you think Maggie is growing fonder for you as a husband?" Henry asked me.

"I would be surprised if that is the case. So far, I'm glad Marshal Plummer has not returned to put pressure on Maggie to ask one of us to be her husband," I said. When it came to courting, I was in unfamiliar and deep water. I sure could not impress Maggie, as I was too shy and respectful. I was barely inches from drowning in my inexperience, ordinariness, and shortness. I was as dashing a man as a broom is to a floor.

I blurted out to change the subject, "Have you noticed Dutch Daan is looking very pale and tired? I have told him that I think he should sell his claim, sluicing equipment, and irrigation ditch, and return to Holland, where he can rest and relax and restore his health.

"Yes, I have noticed Daan's shortness of breath and trouble concentrating. I wonder if he is concerned about Lemon Jim and Frenchy and his brother coming for his gold. It is one thing to obtain gold but quite another to keep it once people know you have it," Henry answered.

CF appeared out of nowhere as Henry and I were talking beside the sluicing machine. He commented, "Dutch Daan have chest pains. I see him clutch his chest often. He try to act like, he not sick."

I said to CF, "Well, you work with him more than we do at the ditch, so we haven't seen his clutching his chest. I think we will all have to have a talk with Daan about his health."

We might have discussed it more but Jacque, Mean Mike, and Dutch Daan joined us at the worksite, and King alerted us that someone was close by. It was Constable Dunn with a big, rough-looking man wearing a badge. The constable introduced us to Marshal Plummer, who had heard that at one time a small Scottish woman had run a food establishment at Hill's Bar. He had checked the lead out with no luck, and now the constable had offered to show the marshal around Emory Creek and the mining camps around Yale, as people could cross the river from Hill's Bar.

Henry acted as a fascinated Englishman, eager to hear all about law enforcement in Montana. He quickly had the American sheriff boasting about his experiences and fame back home. Henry asked if he could hear more of the marshal's exploits as he and the constable searched the area of Emory for the petite lady with a Scottish accent.

Mean Mike surprised us when he told Marshal Plummer that he and I ran Kelly's Café in Yale, along with a Chinese cook named Wong Lee. Mike invited him to eat there any evening he was in the area and explained that one of was there every other night, as we worked mornings in the sluicing. The marshal said that he might stop for a meal, but he preferred a saloon in the evening for drinks or cards. We said that we understood completely, and he was welcome any time.

When Henry, the constable, and the marshal had left the work-site, he explained that he and I would need to work in the café every other day until the marshal moved on. Maggie would need to stay in the kitchen out of sight, and we would replace her in the café so the marshal would not meet her in person. If Maggie would not agree to stay in the kitchen, we would have to encourage her to stay at our camp until the marshal left. Hopefully, that would be a task we didn't have to insist on.

I told Mike that I suspected he really wanted Maggie to ask him to marry her. Mean Mike said, "A true Scotsman never tells what is under his kilt or his intentions concerning a beautiful lass."

I responded with, "Why would Maggie want a big ox like you? One misstep and you could break her foot. And if you rolled on her in your sleep, you would squash the poor lass to death."

"May Maggie pick the best man for her, and it might not be you or me but Henry," Mean Mike said with a big grin and left to work at the café.

I was surprised that Dutch Daan did not get upset when Mean Mike left. He said to Jacque and CF, "Henry will be back before long to help you. I need to talk with Nothing at my camp for a few minutes, and then he will also be back to help with the sluicing."

At his camp, Dutch Daan confided that he was not feeling well. We discussed his extreme tiredness, shortness of breath, chest pains, and lack of concentration. A quick check of his pulse showed it was slightly erratic. I suggested he rest, and I would return in a while with my doctor's bag and check him more thoroughly. I advised him to get lots of rest, and he did not argue. I covered him with his blanket, and he closed his eyes readily.

As I was returning from Dutch Daan's campsite, I could hear King barbing loudly, and I wondered what was going on. The noise was coming from south of our sluicing worksite and heading quickly in that direction.

When I got back to our sluicing site, I saw that King had Frenchy's brother up a tree out of reach and Frenchy in front of the tree with his hands in the air, afraid to move lest King may attack him. Lemon Jim was crouched over Mean Mike on the ground, trying to choke the life out of him.

I ran to Lemon Jim and pounded his ears with my fists. Then, I gouged at his eyes, but Lemon Jim was shaking his head, and I missed injuring him. Next, I grabbed his hair and yanked with every ounce of strength that I had, pulling long strands out of his head.

Lemon Jim had stopped choking Mean Mike and because of my assault to his head, he was struggling to stand up from his crouch. So, I shouldered him, and it was like hitting a wall, but it did knock Lemon Jim off balance, and he fell to his knees on the ground.

Thankfully, Mean Mike had managed to get to his feet, and he staggered and dropped seat first on Lemon Jim's back. Lemon Jim crumbled to the ground under Mike's weight and was motionless as Jacque and CF arrived. They released Frenchy and his brother from King's arrest at the tree and tied the three men's hands behind their backs, while Mean Mike staggered around, shaken, and dazed from his struggle to stay alive. Not knowing if the constable and the marshal would return to our camp, we took our captives to the constable's canoe at the river's edge.

While we were waiting there, Mike told his tale. He had quite literally run into Frenchy, along with his brother and Lemon Jim, a little distance from our worksite. It was a stand-off at first, as Lemon Jim wanted to talk to Mean Mike about buying King from him. When Mike said that he would only sell King for all the gold in the Fraser, Lemon tried to get King to obey his commands and ordered the dog to come to him. King would not go to him, so Lemon Jim grew outraged at both Mike and the coonhound. Frenchy informed Mike that the three of them were going to our worksite to steal our gold.

When Frenchy and his brother tried to close in on Mean Mike, he ordered King to attack them. Frenchy's brother was not ready for the fast-growling hurricane that was nipping at his legs and hands. He retreated up a tree out of the dog's reach. Then King also began attacking Frenchy, who ran toward the tree his brother had climbed. There they stayed, afraid to move because of the barking, snarling, threatening dog. Meanwhile, Lemon Jim wanted to murder Mean Mike with his bare hands. Every bit of rage and hatred in his soul turned Lemon Jim into a deadly, killing beast.

Mean Mike said, "As viciously as King went after Frenchy and his brother, Lemon Jim came after me, and I was taken by surprise. It's hard to reckon with someone who is intent on killing you no matter what. Being slow witted, it was hard for me to face the truth that I was not going to crawl away from this conflict with my life if I did not fight to kill Lemon Jim myself. I could barely hold my own, and then I was down on the ground with my enemy strangling the breath out of me, and I was feeling myself getting weaker and less able to pry at Lemon Jim's strong hands that were crushing my throat. Nothing's arrival came just in time to save me.

Because I saw Lemon Jim shaking his head above me and suddenly, his hands were less forceful on my throat. I had a surge of air and life and I struggled to get up and away from him. As I stood up, unsteady on my feet, I saw Lemon starting to rise from the ground, and I simply dropped my whole weight on him by sitting on him bum first like he was a chair. It knocked the wind and fight out of him, and I sat there with the wind and fight gone out of me as well. As I sat there, a thought flashed through my mind. What was I doing hunting for gold when my father had already taught me a good trade for any able-bodied man? I thought maybe I had a concussion again, and it was making me silly," Mike said with a puzzled expression.

Henry burst in among us just then, saying I had to come quickly because the marshal was shot. Henry and CF came with me, and Mean Mike and Jacque stayed to guard our prisoners. At one of the sluicing sites, the marshal suspected that a group of Americans were hiding a woman from him. The marshal began threatening and trying to intimidate the men because he wanted to make sure whoever the woman was, she wasn't his murderess.

Constable Dunn tried to keep the situation calm but one of the miners challenged the marshal to a gun fight. The marshal had to accept the ultimatum or leave. Marshal Plummer was not as swift as the miner to draw his gun and shoot, and he was now suffering a gunshot wound, holding on somewhere between life and death. By the time we reached the site, he had left for heaven or hell. Henry, CF, and I went to work when Constable Dunn ordered a burial of the marshal's body. We dug a grave in quick order. The marshal was laid in his grave beside the mining claim, which had turned deadly for him.

Hearing of our captives at the river, Constable Dunn returned with us to arrest Frenchy, his brother, and Lemon Jim. Off and on as we went toward the river and the prisoners, we could hear King howling up a storm. When we reached the Fraser's shore, only Lemon Jim remained of the captives. Mean Mike and Lemon Jim were each tied to a tree with gags in their mouths. Jacque was on the ground, groaning in pain. On inspection, we realized he had been stabbed in the back. Henry was able to tell us that he saw Frenchy and his brother heading for our mining site. The constable and Henry went immediately to check that Dutch Daan was safe.

CF and I began doctoring Jacque, who thankfully had not lost a huge amount of blood. The knife had hit his shoulder blade, and the strike wasn't as deadly as he expected. He struggled to ward off his attacker only to be hit on the head, which landed Jacque on the ground as Frenchy's brother, his attacker, took off. There was no time for more explanations of what had happened, as bullets began to land too close for comfort around us. I tried to shelter Jacque, and CF and King vanished into the trees.

As quickly as the bullets started, they stopped. I waited with Jacque, feeling that a bullet might get us at any second. It seemed to me that the shooters must be getting closer and closer to be able to take such careful aim at us. The freely flowing sweat from my brow stung my eyes, and my heart pounded with the fear of being shot. After what seemed like an eternity, CF returned and said Frenchy and his brother had taken off in their canoe. They had fired at us to cover up their escape near us. They wanted us ducking and hiding. I was relieved that they were gone. I realized I was missing the non-violent way of peace so demanded in my Quaker heritage.

CF untied Mean Mike, who began cursing once the gag was out of his mouth. He was yapping at us because we took too long to get him free. CF, usually unflappable, said, "Shut up, Mike! You were not bleeding on the ground." Mike might have said more but Henry and the constable appeared, in response to hearing shots fired. When they arrived, I left to get my doctor's bag so I could treat Henry's knife wound more thoroughly. Henry came with me but left partway to go to check on Dutch Daan at his camp. He would report if Daan was okay. I returned to the shore of the Fraser with my large doctor's bag and completed stitching and bandaging Jacque's injury. He was able to stand and walk about slowly.

When Henry returned with Dutch Daan, the constable was eager to get Lemon Jim to jail. We agreed the constable would paddle his canoe with Lemon Jim as his captive, and I would ride with them, a pistol pointed at Lemon Jim in case he was not co-operative and threatened to overturn the canoe and drown himself rather than face going to jail. Mike would follow us in one of our canoes so he would be close by to help if Lemon Jim went berserk on the journey. Jacque would be helped back to camp by CF, and Henry and Dutch Dan would return to the work of sluicing while Jacque rested.

The canoe trip to Yale and the jailing of Lemon Jim went without any problems. With Lemon Jim behind bars, Mike and I went to share with Maggie that Marshal Plummer would not be a threat to her any longer. She was strangely quiet upon hearing the marshal was dead and buried. We assured Maggie that Henry and both of us were still hoping she would ask one of us to marry her. She gave us a tiny smile and said, "I'll see about that matter very soon." Then she mumbled, "I'm needed in the kitchen," and she disappeared and did not return. She sent Wong Lee out to see if we wanted food. We had the stew but left the café with indigestion at Maggie's strange behavior.

On the return to Emory for our camp and sluicing site, Mike explained how Frenchy and his brother were rescued from being our prisoners tied to trees. Mike explained, "While Jacque and me be waiting with the prisoners, two men arrived in a canoe and came ashore. They said they were looking for the constable and were very friendly and made a fuss over King. They said it was urgent that they contact the constable and asked if one of us could take a message to him. Jacque offered to deliver the message and bring back a response.

The two men asked me if King was good for hunting and when I said he was an excellent hunting dog, they offered to buy him from me. One of them carried a pouch, and he wanted to show me a trophy that his own hunting dog had won. He asked me to look in

the pouch to see the championship cup. As I focused on the contents
of the bag, I felt a gun barrel in my back, and I was directed to a tree,
tied up, and gagged.

They tried to capture King, but he ran off into the woods. The
two men were there because Frenchy and his brother had offered to
sell King to them if they liked the look of the hound. Frenchy and
his brother each tied to a tree, assured the men that all they needed
to do was untie them and they would sell King to them. Impressed
with the dog, the two men untied Frenchy and his brother.

Frenchy and his brother took off to find King in the woods, and
the men waited for them to return. It did not take King long to send
Frenchy and his brother running back into camp, the dog nipping at
their feet and legs. As fast as King sent the French men running into
camp, he was gone again into the woods. The two men who came to
buy King were disgusted with Frenchy and his brother and said they
were leaving. Levelling their guns at the French men, they left.

Lemon Jim was yelling that he needed to be untied, but Frenchy
put a gag in his mouth. Frenchy instructed his brother to search
Lemon Jim's pockets and take anything of value on him. Lemon
Jim was left without his money, ring, watch, and a costly knife from
his boot. Sensing a slight noise, the two brothers scattered. Seeing
Lemon Jim being robbed made me smile. He'll need to work with
better gangsters when he got out of jail.

Jacque returned to us soon after, carrying the water-soaked,
spoiled message for the constable. In his effort to hurry, Jacque had
slipped and dropped the envelope. He had to fish it out of a stream,
and he quickly returned to get another message to take for the constable. As Jacque came near, he realized the men were gone and that
Frenchy and his brother were not tied to the trees, but I was.

Jacque was confused, and he thought that he heard a stirring
behind him, so he turned to see who was there. Frenchy's brother
shrieked and stabbed him in the back. King, lurking near us in the

trees, came thundering and snarling and nipping at the two French men. Frenchy's brother stabbed at King with the knife and struck the dog, who yelped in pain and retreated. Frenchy yelled at his brother to take our guns and come on so they could rob Dutch Daan. They left Jacque on the ground, wounded. King returned shortly and licked Jacque's face, and he sat between me and Jacque, guarding us. There was a patch of blood on the dog's shoulder. He began his mournful howling that lasted off and on until you guys showed up."

I asked Mike if King was badly hurt, and Mike said that he needed to check his knife wound more carefully when we reached camp. It was the first thing Mike did when we got there. King had a knife gash not deep but about three inches long. I insisted we shave the hair around the cut and clean it and treat it with iodine. The cut did not need stitches. By the time the hair grew back around the wound, hopefully it would be well healed. Until then, we would make sure it did not get infected. King accepted all his attention in this regard as due him. That night we sat around the campfire, everyone in shock at the events of the day. Most days are routine, even a touch boring, but there are some in which things stampede about us, and we feel runover and not sure what we should think. CF said, "Today we fall off cliff but land on our feet." We all agreed.

CHAPTER SIXTEEN:

Gold—Not Enough to Hold us Together

IN THE SECOND month of our agreement, Dutch Daan suffered enough heart trouble to set his mind on selling his sluicing equipment, irrigation ditch, and mining stake at Emory. He assured us that he would try to make this happen as quickly as possible, and then our partnership would end. We agreed to work for him until he sold out. Dutch Daan was eager to return to Holland. We encouraged him to sell to the first honest buyer, as more gold or a better price would not help his heart condition.

In the third month of our sluicing, Alf and Dino returned to Yale and checked in with us at Emory. They actually wanted Jacque and CF to join up with them in guiding people into the gold strikes that were inland in the Cariboo region. Jacque was familiar with Fort Alexandria and the general Cariboo area, which included the Fraser River Plateau with the Coast Mountains on the west and the Cariboo Mountains on the east. It was an expanse of grassland, forests, numerous lakes, and several rivers beside the Fraser, such as the Quesnel, Cariboo, Chilcotin, and Horsefly. It was the home of grizzlies, moose, and mule deer. Jacque had found in the past that two of three native peoples from the area were open to fur trading, whereas The Tsilhqot'in native people in the same area had not been interested in trade

Jacque was ready to join Alf and Dino as soon as possible in guiding rather than sluicing for gold. CF preferred to return to his mother's people and to work at the Hudson's Bay Company fort at Kamloops. Dutch Dan offered Jacque the chance to leave the sluicing and go with Alf and Dino right away, which Jacque was glad to take.

All of us had a healthy stash of gold and searching for more was over for the five of us. I knew I had a life as a fully trained doctor to pursue, maybe with a wife. Henry had a family title and estate to manage back in England, also maybe with a beautiful wife. Mean Mike had decided that there was always work for a blacksmith, and he had the means for a forge. Maggie knew soon our group would be no more and that two of us hoped she would marry one of us.

CF wanted to stay at the sluicing until it was over, then he was certain he could return to his people on his own. Dutch Daan suggested that CF instead return to Holland with him to help him travel in his poor health. If CF did so, Henry wanted him to come to his estate in England for a visit. CF was excited at seeing more 'White people places,' and he trusted both Dutch Daan and Henry, so he was open to the adventure. Jacque asked CF to talk to his mother and get her permission for his travels. CF promised Jacque that he would. Jacque left with Alf and Dino. We all knew it was what his heart craved, being in the unspoiled wilderness.

Some men cannot be tamed, they will not stay long in a herd. They will always be their own person. Jacque had that independent free French blood in his veins from his ancestors as runners of the woods, mixed with the Aboriginal blood of the people of the land. He felt at home hunting, trapping, and being in pristine nature. He understood that the mountains themselves would limit settlements, roads, and towns. He was content to guide men hungry for gold, men ready to build roads, eager to build towns, and straining to farm valleys, but he would spend much of his life retreating to his own slices of wilderness, ever content there.

Word spread quickly that Dutch Daan wanted to sell his mining claim and equipment, and several people seemed eager. Dutch Daan said if it did not sell in a month, he would hold an auction. Three buyers quickly tried to get Daan to accept their offer, fearing they might pay more if the claim, equipment, and irrigation ditch were bought separately at auction. A man named Horace Wapoh bought everything from Dutch Daan and was ready to take over on the site on the twenty-second of October.

The last three weeks meant facing our separation as friends and partners, which was bittersweet. None of us would be sorry to stop sluicing. The amount of gold our mining operation had produced was more than a sizable nest egg for each of us, and yet the gold rush fever had never consumed us. Faro dealer Smith was right about us, as we were not obsessed with finding gold. Our desire was staying alive and taking care of each other. We were willing to share any gold found and were not about each man for himself. It was an adventure that was not worth anyone's death to get rich.

Maggie Kelly invited the four of us and Daan to a special meal at the café. She promised to ask one of the two of us to marry her or none of us. I did not know if I would be asked to marry Maggie, but I tried not to dwell on it. It was the closest I had ever been to having a wife, and I was trying to not be devastated about Maggie's decision if she didn't choose me. I was sure the meal was delicious, but it could have been sawdust, as I was tied in knots both in my stomach and my mind. I could not tell how Henry was feeling, but I was like a tightly strung fiddle string ready to break at any second.

Dutch Daan surprised us all when he presented Maggie with a pouch of gold dust. He said she had made life for all of us sparkle, and her food had warmed our stomachs and souls. Maggie was visibly touched by such an unexpected gift. CF warned Maggie that I was bossy, and Henry did not carry a gun or knife but an iron and ironing board.

Maggie said with a sad smile, "Since Marshal Plummer is no longer a threat to me, I do not need a husband. I do thank each of you Henry, Nothing, for wanting me to ask you to marry me. Henry, I cannot ask you to marry me because one of the issues with my first marriage was that I could not have children. Henry, as part of English nobility your wife must bear you heirs. You're a kind and wonderful man, but I would be out of place in a British estate. You know yourself I would be a cat in the hen house. I wish you a happy marriage in England and many sons who can sing like you."

Henry, always a gentleman and considerate of others, said to Maggie. "I shall remember you always as the beautiful lady who would have been a rose in my life of British nobility. Whoever you marry is a fortunate man! I wish you great happiness."

Maggie said, "Nothing Brown, you are short but very tall in my mind. Your honor and respect have deeply impressed me. And . . . it has shown me that I need you to marry me and Wong Lee officially before God, as we have been secretly living as husband and wife for some years now."

My heart and mind stalled. I stammered and sputtered, "You have been living as spouses but without having had a marriage ceremony? You are asking me as a preacher to marry you and Wong Lee so you will be officially married? You want God's blessing on you as husband and wife?"

"Yes, I want God to bless Wong Lee as my husband, as he was a savior to me. I want to vow my love to him before God and you my friends before you scatter away. I ask you all to be witnesses to our marriage so that you can swear I pledged to love and honor him and that I vowed not to shoot him like my first husband," Maggie said sincerely and honestly.

Mean Mike asked Maggie, "How was Wong Lee your savior?"

"He found me savagely beaten beside my husband's dead body. Although, I shot my husband, I was too battered to crawl away. Wong Lee had heard the shot as he was delivering laundry to our house, and he looked to see if something was wrong. When he saw me bleeding, my black and blue face, one eye swollen shut, and not caring if I lived or died, Wong Lee took pity on me and hid me in his cart. He cared for me secretly at his family's laundry. After I mostly healed, we left town to escape Marshal Plummer, my brother-in-law, and have operated cafés following gold rushes, first in California and now here. To the world, I am a White woman running establishments with a Chinese cook. It will always seem that way to most people, but at least God and you five will know better. I trust you Nothing, as both a friend and man of God. Will you marry us, right here, right now?" Maggie demanded of me.

I answered, "Of course I will." This caused a response of cheers of approval from the others. The wedding was simple, with Maggie and Wong Lee totally invested in loving and caring for each other as long as they both should live. We were all happy for the couple and their love, but yet aching inside that we were all soon parting ways. Friendship, acceptance, trust, and respect were more valuable to all of us than gold. Loneliness squeezes the life out of people, like the wilderness where no one is home for miles and miles.

It wasn't long after the official wedding of Maggie and Wong Lee that we divided our last shares of gold and began the next directions of our lives. My journey to becoming a fully trained doctor began in Victoria, assisting Doctor John. Thanks to Judge Begbie, who I remained able to keep in contact with over the years, I learned of those who I partnered with along the Fraser.

Henry became a responsible duke in England and still carried his pitch pipe. He directed polished and talented choirs, as well.

Jacque continued to be sought after as a wilderness guide in the growing colony.

CF traveled to Holland with Dutch Daan and stayed with him, as he was quite weak and ill. Dutch Dan died after six months, leaving half of his wealth to CF. After Dutch Daan's death, CF spent time with Henry in England and was tutored and able to work in business there. He worked for the Hudson's Bay Company in the London office, rising to a high position.

Mean Mike remained in Yale and set up a blacksmith shop. He became a partner in mule trains delivering supplies into the interior of the colony. As time progressed, he was also the driver of a stage line from Yale, running clear up to Barkerville in the Cariboo region. He continued to be in the company of lovely ladies, but he never married. He often said he didn't need a wife because he had King, the blue tick coonhound that men have died to own.

And our colorful friend Judge Begbie was knighted by the queen for his service in the development of British Columbia.

Author's Postscript: I watch the mighty Fraser River today, over a century and a half later, still flowing as powerfully and as dangerously as ever. It knows like its neighboring mountains and valleys that they will never be tamed by mere human beings in all their arrogance and attempts to control, develop, and subdue them. I believe those known as The Deadly Five and The Second Five understood this truth.

ABOUT THE AUTHOR

RAYMOND MAHER SEES himself as a storyteller. In both of his professions before retirement—teacher and ordained minister—the art of storytelling was critical to gain interest and motivate learning and enjoyment.

With a lifelong passion for the history of Canada, his study of the Fraser River Gold Rush of 1858 was the catalyst for his first novel, *The Deadly Five*, which was published in 2020.

Maher has worked and lived in four different Canadian provinces, experiencing the disadvantage of being a stranger in town. Thus, his writing reflects the need for acceptance, trust, recognition, and humor. These are evident in his novels and weekly newspaper columns.

Raymond's most recent literary award was Honorable Mention in the Inspirational or Spiritual category for "A Cuckoo on the Street," 2021 Writer's Digest Magazine 90th Annual Competition.

He lives in Chilliwack, British Columbia, Canada, near the historic Five Corners, with his spouse of over fifty-five years.

You can find out more about the author at:
www.raymondmaher.com, Raymond Maher-Author-Facebook, and According to Ed website newspaper columns.

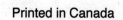
Printed in Canada